COMES A HORSEMAN

When John Dancer rides into Matchstick, everyone knows there's trouble ahead. Brian Solon, owner of the huge SS ranch, figures he's there to help the small ranchers along the river; some believe he's there to aid Esperanza Del Rio, who has a tenuous claim on Solon's land; and debt-ridden banker Sanford Wilkes' guilty conscience over embezzled funds gives him cause to panic at Dancer's appearance. And then someone goes to the extreme of hiring Mad Jack Doyle to murder Dancer . . .

Books by C. J. Sommers
in the Linford Western Library:

GHOST RANCH

C. J. Sommers

COMES A HORSEMAN

Complete and Unabridged

LINFORD
Leicester

First published in Great Britain in 2011 by
Robert Hale Limited
London

First Linford Edition
published 2013
by arrangement with
Robert Hale Limited
London

A catalogue record for this book is available
from the British Library.

ISBN 978–1–4448–1743–0

Published by
F. A. Thorpe (Publishing)
Anstey, Leicestershire

Set by Words & Graphics Ltd.
Anstey, Leicestershire
Printed and bound in Great Britain by
T. J. International Ltd., Padstow, Cornwall

This book is printed on acid-free paper

1

Dancer was the man's name, or what he called himself. If he had another name no one knew what it was. He came in off the desert one broiling hot day riding a big bay horse with a black mane and tail, and a few heads were raised to watch him as he entered the town of Matchstick. Passing a crudely made barn at the outskirts of Matchstick he was observed by two men working there. They noticed that he carried two scabbards for his Henry repeating rifles, one on either side of his saddle, also that two Colt revolvers decorated his hips. There was a third, empty holster at the back of his belt.

'He don't want that one jolting out while he's riding,' Drew Tucker told his younger cousin.

'He looks like he's going off to war,' Harvey Tucker said.

'Wherever he goes there's likely to be a war,' Drew answered. 'That is one bad man and the only thing to do is stay well clear of him.'

Doretta (Dottie) Lang was sweeping off the porch in front of Nichols' General Store when she saw the stranger ride into town. She straightened up, putting a hand at the base of her spine. Dottie Lang was six months pregnant and the work was getting harder for her. Most people thought that clerking in a store was a soft job, but they forgot the shelving of items, the constant clean-up, the bending and stretching. She didn't hate Tyne Nichols, after all, he had given her a job when she sorely needed one, but he was not an easy man to work for with his constant fussing and cursing.

Yes, she needed the job — the bank was threatening to foreclose on the tiny twenty-five acre ranch she and her husband, Tom, shared. Tom worked from sunup to sundown as Dottie did when she was at the ranch, but they had no ready cash and a baby on the way and so Dottie had taken the job in Matchstick to try to save enough for present and future expenses.

As the rider approached the store, which was on the very outskirts of Matchstick, Dottie looked up to examine him, as one did with every stranger in this remote part of the country. He was tall, wearing a buckskin jacket over a yellow silk shirt. He glanced her way and she saw that his eyes were a soft gray, yet expressionless and cold enough to pierce through the heart. She thought, 'This is a man who will not stand for being insulted or lied to.' She had to turn her own eyes away from his stare and return to her chore.

Whoever he was, she knew instinctively, that he was a very hard man.

Porky Bing who worked at the Come Along Stable saw the tall man on the bay horse kicking up a stream of light dust as he approached. Being a stableman by nature and profession, he appreciated the depth and muscle of the bay's chest and looked instinctively at the brand on its right flank: XO, a well-known Texas brand. So the stranger with the cold eyes was a visitor, or only passing through.

Or just maybe, Bing thought as he studied the way the man was set up and how he was armed, he had some serious business to conduct in Matchstick.

'I'll be leaving my saddle. I know you'll keep an eye on it.' That sounded more like an order than a request to Bing.

He saw Dancer pull a pistol wrapped in oilskin from his saddle-bags, unwrap it, and tuck it into the holster riding on the back of his belt. *What does a man want with three pistols?* Bing wondered. It had been common in the West years ago when cap-and-ball pistols took so much longer to reload, and when the Indian menace was much greater. Men then had carried three, four pistols, even more. Perhaps the tall man had carried over the habit — or, Bing speculated — maybe he was in the kind of business that required a lot of firepower.

As he watched, the tall man slid both of his Henry rifles from their scabbards and tucked them under one arm.

'Do you happen to know of a good hotel?' Dancer asked.

'Yes, sir. There's the Silver Palace, three blocks up on the south side of the street.'

Dancer nodded and left the stable. Bing found that his heart slowed a little. He did not care for being in that man's presence.

* * *

'Well, what's he here for!' Brian Solon demanded of the town marshal.

'I don't know,' Royce Peebles said evenly. 'Besides we don't even know that it's Dancer.'

'That's what people are saying,' the angry Brian Solon said. Solon was not only the owner of the huge SS ranch south of Matchstick, but the man who virtually controlled the politics of Cameron County, as was frequently the case in cattle country where the economy was based on big ranches. Marshal Peebles had not seen the cattleman this concerned since he had discovered three local men with running irons changing his brand to their own legally registered 88 mark two years earlier. Then Solon had threatened to change his own brand to something unprintable. The threat was never carried out, of course, because Brian Solon was running about 6,000 head of cattle on his wide-spreading range, and the work would have taken a staggering amount of time. Brian Solon was not a man who liked to waste time or money.

'Well, you had better find out who he is for sure — and if it is Dancer, find out what he is doing here,' Solon ordered.

'I'll do my best,' Peebles answered, which was not a firm enough response for Brian Solon.

'Do it, or I'll have your badge,' Solon threatened before he put on his hat and stalked out the door, banging it shut as he passed through.

Peebles sat behind his desk, boots propped up and chewed his mustache while he pondered his orders. He did wear a badge and it wouldn't seem out of the ordinary to ask a man for his name, but it would be a little like demanding that Mysterious Dave Mather tell him what he was up to. Those types of men didn't take kindly to prying. And their reactions were often volatile.

Considering further, as the marshal pared his fingernails with a pocketknife, Peebles thought he could simply find the man with his back turned and say, 'Mr Dancer?' Of course, that could provoke the response of a drawn pistol if the man happened to be jittery on that particular morning. If the man was Dancer at all — who was to say he was? Few people knew Dancer. Few who were still alive. Probably it was only a rumor that had started in some saloon.

That didn't calm Peebles's nerves at all. He was not a lawman by inclination, but out of necessity. He had developed a fondness for eating. Sighing, he folded his knife and rose. He would begin with the stables — the man must have left his horse somewhere; if not he was simply halting for a drink or provisions and would be on his way soon whether Peebles talked to him or not.

Somehow the marshal did not feel that Dancer was leaving soon. He was here with some aim in mind. The question was, *what?*

*   *   *

Sanford Wilkes was at work in the small bank he owned. His teller, Porter Hall, had taken a lunch break. Wilkes was crouched in front of the small safe in his office, sweat beading his bald head, his small eyes over-excited. He had heard the rumor — Dancer was in

Matchstick. Why? How could anyone have known about the stolen bank assets? Yet someone must have summoned the man. One of his depositors? That seemed improbable, yet the badman had descended on Matchstick for some purpose. Sanford Wilkes was perspiring profusely. He counted the bills and gold in his vault once, twice and began again . . . he could not have embezzled that much money! Yet the evidence said that he had.

It had begun with chipping $500 from a depositor's money to buy his wife a new carriage she coveted. That was a year ago. Agatha was one of those banker's wives who had the strange idea that since her husband worked in a bank around all that money, he must necessarily be wealthy himself. It was the only reason she had agreed to marry the short, balding man. When the life she was forced to lead proved to be less than that of her dreams, Agatha felt deprived; she thought her husband parsimonious. With all of his money she was expected to get by on a paltry twenty-dollar a month allowance. Why, the mayor's wife, Flora, was budgeted double that, Agatha happened to know. How was she to keep up appearances on such a stingy stipend?

She felt that Sanford was misusing her, and so she pled for more money. And pled. Her nagging did the trick, she was happy to discover, and her own allowance doubled and then tripled after she had made it clear to Sanford that she was suffering at his hands and would not put up with it long. Since it had worked once, it became a regular habit of Agatha's and she increased her demands and the volume of same until Sanford had started staying away from home more frequently.

That habit had led him to spending more time at the Blue Ribbon saloon where out of boredom he had begun to drink more and gamble heavily at the roulette table. Of course he lost more than he won, but he was able to sustain his habit by using the same method as he used to finance Agatha's whims. At one point he had sat down with pencil and paper and estimated that he owed the bank — that is, everyone in town — a total of $5,700.

That did not stop Sanford Wilkes, or even slow him down, though he did anguish a little more when an even number instead of an odd one came up on the roulette wheel. As with all habits, it was much easier to acquire them than to break. Yet, there always comes a day of reckoning, does there not? He was convinced that this had come on the day that Dancer rode into Matchstick, although he could not have said what made him so certain. Maybe it was a simple case of nerves or an attack of conscience.

He had been planning to foreclose on certain of the small ranchers and sell their properties for a quick infusion of funds, disguising his embezzlement with the new money, but there hadn't been time for the plan to reach fruition. What Sanford Wilkes was thinking at this moment was how to slip away quietly from Matchstick before he was imprisoned.

* * *

The knock on the door brought Dancer's head up from the task at hand. He had disassembled two pistols and was busy cleaning the trail dust from them and oiling them. His third revolver, which had been protected by oilskin and carried in his saddlebags, rested close at hand on the table of his second-floor room in the Silver Palace Hotel. He quietly cocked it and walked to the door, his gun hand behind his back. He did not think he had any enemies in Matchstick, but that did not mean there was none. He opened the door to find a mustached man with neatly parted pomaded hair and a silver badge glistening on the front of his black shirt.

'Mind if I come in, Dancer?' Marshal Royce Peebles asked.

Dancer frowned. He did not like the fact that the lawman knew his name and where to find him. He did not like the fact that his arrival in town had been noted. He shrugged his broad shoulders, though, simply said, 'I don't mind,' and returned to the table where he placed his third revolver within reach, a point not unobserved by Marshal Peebles. 'What's on your mind?' he asked Royce Peebles.

Peebles had taken the only other chair in the room, pulled it near the table and seated himself.

'Mostly what you're up to,' Peebles said, his voice a little thin as he found himself across the table from the noted badman. He tried to put a little more force in his words, yet appear at the same time to be friendly. Dancer's hard gray eyes were without expression, but it seemed to Peebles that they bored into him.

Peebles cleared his throat and tried a smile. 'What it is, is a few people around here are concerned that a gunfighter has been hired to do work for those who might have it in for them.'

Dancer didn't even bother to answer. He had begun to reassemble one of the blue-steel Colts resting on the table.

'If I could explain further what the local situation is . . . ' Peebles said. Dancer looked up and met the town marshal's eyes again as he slapped the cylinder into the clean, reassembled pistol. With some uneasiness Peebles continued:

'One of our local ranchers is at odds with a number of small settlers whose holdings have closed his corridor to the Chickasaw Creek, where his cattle are normally watered. Especially now, with this drought we've been having . . . he needs that water. The wells he's dug are not enough for the number of steers he runs.'

Dancer realized that he was expected to say something, but what could he say? He did not care about the squabbling of local ranchers. 'Tell him to buy 'em out,' was Dancer's best advice.

'It would take a lot of cash which Mr Solon will not have until round-up time, and some of the small ranchers are so stubborn that it seems they wouldn't take double the worth of the land they claim. And Solon won't have even fair-market price to pay them if his cattle start dying on him for lack of water.'

Dancer, whose hand had been busy all the while, only shrugged again. He was now reloading the second pistol, holstering it as he finished. Dancer rose to his feet and stared down at Marshal Peebles with that cold gaze of his.

'What has any of this to do with me?' he demanded softly.

'Well some people — Mr Solon, that is — seem to have the idea that the small ranchers have banded together and have hired a professional gunman to come in here and take care of business.'

'Is that what you think I am?' Dancer

asked. 'A professional gunman?'

There was something like a muted challenge in his voice and Peebles didn't feel at all comfortable sitting there any more. He fabricated an answer. 'You know how people are. I mean, obviously you aren't a lawman.'

'Why obviously?' Dancer asked.

'Well, you don't wear a badge,' Peebles replied shakily.

'A badge is a way of advertising who you are. Useful in trying to assert your authority — say in trying to break up a bar brawl, but of little use if you're trying to get things accomplished without letting people know they might be under suspicion.'

'Then you are . . . ?'

'Whatever I am, it's of no interest to you, and frankly none of your business.'

Dancer crossed the wooden floor and swung the door wide. 'I'm a little trail-weary, Marshal. Now, if you don't mind, I am going to hit that bed over there and sleep for as many hours as I can.'

Peebles nodded, rose from his chair and walked out into the corridor, realizing that he had learned absolutely nothing about Dancer and his plans.

John Dancer — for that was his full name, one he did not give out because he didn't want anyone feeling that he was that close to them — locked the door and crossed to the bed. After removing his boots he stared up at the ceiling for a while as the sky grew dark beyond the window and the peace of the day was overtaken by the urgent, bawdy sounds of the night in this small border town.

⋆ ⋆ ⋆

Esperanza del Rio's eyes flickered toward the doorway of the Blue Ribbon Saloon as the six men trooped in noisily. They were all riders for the SS ranch, Brian Solon's spread. Except it was not Brian Solon's land. Esperanza's black eyes sparked with hatred. The SS land belonged to her family; it always

17

had. King Philip IV of Spain had awarded the land grant to her ancestor, Domingo del Rio in recognition of his service to his country. Esperanza had grown up with this knowledge and every male member of the del Rio family had sworn to retake the land. As time went by and Spanish power had waned, and the Mexicans had been overwhelmed by a new dynasty of empire-builders, her faith had waned, but not her fervor.

Secretly she disliked the Mexicans as well — they were the ones who had first challenged her family's right to the Spanish land, claiming that after the revolution it was now all a part of Mexico. But the Mexicans had made no use of the land and their own claim was eventually forgotten. Not so with the Americans, who continued to emigrate westward, devouring land as they came. Esperanza now worked serving tables in this stinking saloon, giving beer and a false smile to the robbers who had deprived her of her birthright. It was a demeaning decline for her and her family.

There were two new arrivals whom she found particularly disgusting, and they were both among the group who had just entered the Blue Ribbon. Bull Brody was a man who looked like a pig and smelled like one as well. If he were stripped and thrown into a hog pen no one would notice his presence, although the pigs would probably move away from his stink. Reno Marke was the other man she disliked violently — he was young and good-looking enough but he seemed to think that he was an Adonis. He was always preening and posing. He could not keep his eyes or hands away from Esperanza, not seeming to understand that she did not like the vain young man. He always smelled strongly of bay rum and took any chance to brush up against Esperanza as she passed him. He did it again as they walked past her and elbowed their way up to the crowded bar.

She sometimes thought about purchasing a gun for the sole purpose of killing the young blond SS rider, yet this was not Spain and no jury would understand her motive. She walked slowly to the table where the SS riders were seated and took their orders, trying to ignore the stares and lingering touch of Reno Marke's hand on her upper leg.

*   *   *

Tom Lang had finished fitting and nailing on the horseshoes to the last of his fractious colts. The twelve young horses had no idea what was happening to them and they resisted his attentions in a variety of ways. He had made it through the day with having only once been bitten and twice been kicked. One kick on the thigh, one which grazed his cheek with a powerfully launched hoof, but he had wrestled with them — a light-weight against a pack of heavy-weights. Only his determination had let him win the encounters. Those ponies, born wild, were now ready for sale, and represented a small fortune.

Tom rose from the stool he had been sitting on and placed his tools away. Outside the barn a low orange sun was settling behind the hills. It would be dark before long and he still had to harness the team to the buckboard for the trip into town to bring Dottie back to the ranch. With a deep, aggravated shrug, he removed his leather apron. His jawbone was throbbing and a lump was developing there. His leg, he had discovered earlier, had a huge purple bruise on the inside of his thigh. It had been a rough day, but no more difficult than many others. It had to be done if he were to somehow make a living off his twenty-five dry acres, which he had to do — for Dottie's sake and for the sake of his unborn son . . . or daughter.

Brian Solon did not want him to succeed; he did not want any of the small ranchers in the valley to succeed. He wanted them to fail and blow away in the desert wind. The owner of the SS already had all of the land he could use, but he was adamant about needing a corridor through their land to the Chickasaw Creek to water his cattle. There was another trail leading to the river, but it was roundabout and needed at least two days' work from his hired hands to reach it with the huge herd of cattle that the SS ran. Two days was too long for Solon, who was an impatient man, and so for the last three years he had simply instructed his men to drive the cattle to water straight through the land belonging to Tom Lang and his neighbors.

Feelings had run high, but Solon had them outnumbered at least two to one. The law was no help — Marshal Peebles was obviously in Solon's pocket.

Tom stepped out of the barn into the cool of the evening. And now this — his nearest neighbor, Esteban Cruz, who had vowed to help Tom band the other small ranchers together, string wire if necessary to prevent Solon from driving his steers across their land, had returned from Matchstick to advise Tom that Solon had brought in a hired killer to do his dirty work for him.

'This man, Dancer, is *malo*,' Esteban had said in his extremely accented English. 'A very bad man. He will kill us, I think, one by one.'

Except he wouldn't, Tom vowed. First he needed to get Dottie out of Matchstick, away from the danger, and then he would find a way to protect her from the notorious Dancer. Then he would take the fight to its origin, to Brian Solon's doorstep.

2

Night was settling over Matchstick, the heat fading as if the diamond stars above were a cooling force. Inside the Blue Ribbon saloon it was much warmer. The closely packed bodies, the flickering lamps, the tobacco wreaths all seemed to combine to overheat the small building. That was certainly the way it felt to Esperanza. The SS riders had scooted from the crowded bar and taken a table in the small nook next to one of the front windows of the Blue Ribbon. As she passed them, carrying a tray, they began pounding on the table, calling out to her for service. Esperanza glanced that way but did not offer them a smile or a nod. She wore a colorfully striped flaring skirt and an off-the-shoulders white blouse this evening; her glossy black hair was pinned up.

After delivering her tray of drinks to

the gamblers around the roulette wheel, she tugged the material of her blouse up over her smooth brown shoulders, sighed inaudibly and returned to the cowboys' table. Esperanza noticed a tall man in a yellow silk shirt entering through the green door of the Blue Ribbon as she passed. His cold gray eyes followed her briefly, then flickered to the bar and the gambling area. Esperanza was sure she had never seen the man before, but somehow it seemed that he knew her.

'About time,' Bull Brody said as Esperanza reached their tables. 'Look at these empty mugs! A man could die of thirst around here.'

'Same again?' Esperanza asked stiffly. There was no way to avoid getting close enough to Reno Marke so that he was able to run a hand along her leg.

'You have anything on special?' the blond man asked, letting his hand stray again.

'No!' Esperanza shouted so that heads turned her way. She slapped

Reno Marke's hand away and spun back toward the bar, but Reno grabbed her arm roughly and pulled her back.

'Why are you always in so much of a hurry?' he demanded. Across from him the bulky, savage-looking Bull Brody grinned with delight.

'Being around you always makes me hurry,' Esperanza said. 'Hurry away.'

'Leave the girl alone,' an unfamiliar voice said, and a strong hand was clamped around Reno Marke's wrist. Reno turned his head to see a tall man in a yellow silk shirt. Cold gray eyes met his. Reluctantly Reno let Esperanza go.

Rubbing his wrist, Reno saw the twin Colt revolvers the man wore. Those disconcerting eyes continued to bore into him. A glance at his drinking companions revealed that they expected Reno to do something about the situation, so he summoned up enough gumption to snarl and say to Dancer:

'Around here we don't butt into someone's personal business.'

'No?' Dancer's expression hadn't changed. 'Where I come from we don't go around molesting young women.'

'Oh, I was just talking to her,' Reno complained, rubbing his wrist.

Bull Brody, who had been watching with a moody, glowering expression, half-rose from behind the table. 'It looks like I'd better handle this for you, Reno,' said the bearlike man with menace.

'I take care of my own trouble, Bull. Sit down,' Reno said, deciding he could not afford to lose face in front of his companions. Dancer had already started away when the sound of Reno's chair legs scraping against the floor caused him to turn and face the man. Along the bar men stood facing the two in the center of the room. Gambling had briefly stopped at the roulette wheel as players looked their way.

Reno Marke had no idea what he was going to do. As he rose he mentally sorted through his bag of dirty tricks.

Finally he adopted a false smile and approached Dancer with his hands held high and spread apart.

'Look, mister, I'm sorry if . . . ' That was as far as he went, then he tried kicking Dancer in the crotch.

Dancer had been around for a long while. He had seen that particular dirty trick before. Reno's boot met Dancer's crossed wrists and as Dancer took a grip he yanked upward, throwing Reno off balance. Dancer then returned the favor to Reno Marke while his leg was upraised. Dancer's boot caught the young blond man squarely on the crotch and Reno bellowed a pained curse before he hit the floor, clutching himself and half-sobbing.

More quickly than a man his size would seem able to move, Bull Brody rushed toward Dancer, roaring, his fists tightly bunched. Easily Dancer stepped aside and tripped the big man. With a slick, rapid draw, he had his pistol in position to bang the barrel against Bull's skull just behind his ear. The big man crumpled up and hit the floor next to the writhing Reno Marke, out cold.

Dancer's eyes flickered to the table where the men had been seated. He still gripped his pistol. The other four SS riders held their places. Sliding the revolver back into the holster, Dancer nodded to no one and started toward the door. Esperanza ran after him.

At the roulette table, the banker, Sanford Wilkes, had witnessed the entire event. He asked the man beside him, 'Who was that?'

'I don't know.'

'It's the gun hand they call Dancer,' another man told him. 'I heard he was in town.' His eyes flickered toward the door. 'I don't think I'd like to be in his sights.'

'Gentlemen, place your bets!' the croupier barked, but Sanford Wilkes neglected to do so. He was still staring at the closed door, wondering if he was the one in Dancer's sights. He swore to himself that if he was lucky enough to win on this night he would begin replacing the money he had taken from the bank.

Outside in the coolness of evening Dancer paused on his way along the plankwalk as someone, a woman, called out to him. At least it must be him she was calling as there was no one else around.

'Hey, you! Wait a minute!' Esperanza called again, hurrying toward Dancer, her skirts hoisted. Dancer halted and turned toward the girl. Esperanza was breathing heavily when she halted in front of him, holding fingertips to her breast. She spoke in a pant.

'I am so glad you have come. Now that you have helped me, will you continue to do so?' Obsidian eyes gleamed in the starlight as she looked up at him. When Dancer didn't answer, she went on, 'I know who you are — everyone in town does now. Will you help me?'

'I don't think I'm the one to come to for assistance,' Dancer said with the faintest of smiles. 'But, tell me, what do you need help with?'

'What?' Esperanza appeared more than a little surprised. Her voice calmed as her breathing became regular. 'My land, the Rancho Esperanza. They have taken it from me.'

'Who, and when?' Dancer asked calmly.

'This man called Brian Solon. He calls the land his SS ranch.'

'I've heard of him,' Dancer acknowledged. 'You say he stole the land from you?' He wondered if he would have listened this long if the woman were not so attractive. Her hair, which had been pinned up now had a long raven-black tress falling down her shoulder toward her breast. Her mouth was full, her dark eyes attractive and eager.

'Not at first,' Esperanza told him. 'I mean to say that the land belonged to my family for hundreds of years — King Philip himself gave it us. Then you see, the Mexicans came and claimed the land. After the war, the Americans took the land away from the Mexicans, who had taken it from the Spanish.'

Who had taken it from the Indians, Dancer thought but did not say.

'Such a thing could never have happened in Spain to a noble family,' Esperanza said, shaking her head vigorously.

'I wouldn't know — I've never been to Spain,' Dancer replied.

'Neither have I,' she admitted, 'but I know it could not happen there — any more than a man would allow those pigs in the bar to grab at me.' She seemed to shudder a little. 'That's why I followed you. You do not let those SS riders do whatever they please. You are not afraid of them.'

'I don't know what getting into a shooting fight with Brian Solon could possibly profit you,' Dancer had to tell her. 'Why can't you ask the courts to determine who owns the land — if you still have the land grant deed. I was out in California not long ago and I know for a fact that the courts there sided with some families who had claims

32

based on the old Spanish land grants.'

'This is not California,' Esperanza said, her temper returning. 'This is Matchstick, where Solon controls everyone from the judges to the marshal. Besides,' she added in a more somber voice, 'I have no money for a lawyer. What do you think I earn working in a saloon! Nothing. Money for bread, beans and sometimes a little meat. But I have right on my side, don't you see, Dancer?'

'Maybe. The way you are looking at it, but I'm certainly not a lawyer or a judge. I don't know how the law views it.'

'But you will help me, anyway, getting rid of Solon?'

'No, I don't think so,' Dancer said softly. 'I can't afford the trouble right now, and it would probably only make your position weaker.'

Dancer glanced up as a buckboard rolled by. He recognized the pregnant woman as the one he had seen earlier as he entered town. Driving the wagon was a grim-faced young man with fresh bruising on his face.

Esperanza never glanced that way, her black eyes were fixed on Dancer. 'But . . . ' she protested, 'you fought the SS cowboys in the saloon.'

'I fought them for what they were doing, not for who they were,' Dancer said. 'I'm very sorry.'

'You fought for me,' Esperanza said insistently.

'Whoever you were, I would have done the same thing,' Dancer told her. Her challenging eyes met his again, and her lips parted showing fine white teeth, but she said nothing. He did have sympathy for the girl, but not enough to go to war for her. And there was no way he could win with the odds stacked the way they were. He hadn't yet decided whether Esperanza was naïve or manipulative. He thought she was only a pretty young woman disappointed in life, reaching out for any help that might have come her way.

They both turned as the sound of

rapidly approaching boots sounded against the boardwalk. A man was striding quickly toward them. There was a silver marshal's badge on his shirtfront. Royce Peebles halted near them, his face excited.

'I heard there was a commotion at the Blue Ribbon. Do you know anything about it, Dancer?'

'I think that's all over with now, Marshal,' Dancer answered calmly.

'Well . . . ' Peebles said, his eyes showing surprise at the unexpected sight of Dancer and Esperanza del Rio in close conversation. 'I suppose I'd better go there anyway, just to make sure they've calmed down. No one was shot?' he asked Dancer.

'No one fired a gun,' Dancer answered. 'I'd have heard it.'

Just then Sanford Wilkes emerged from the Blue Ribbon, putting his hat on. He glanced at Dancer and the marshal in conversation and felt a small tremor of unease. Both men turned and looked directly at him. The banker hurried away in the opposite direction, feeling their eyes on his back. Wilkes found that he was perspiring though the night had settled to comfortable coolness. He had lost another $400 on the roulette wheel. On this night he had tried doubling up each time he lost, as a strategy. Whoever had thought that up as a way to come away a winner eventually should be taken out and shot.

Who was Dancer, and why were he and the marshal standing in front of the Blue Ribbon in close conversation? It seemed reasonable to conclude that Dancer represented some sort of law enforcement agency, and it was entirely possible that it was the banker himself who interested them. He wondered if his teller, the young Porter Hall, had grown suspicious and decided to talk to the marshal. If so, he would fire the young pup . . . no, that would prompt still more suspicions. Wilkes hurried along through the settling darkness.

Marshal Peebles looked Dancer and

Esperanza over and turned toward the green door to the Blue Ribbon. As he reached it six SS cowboys brushed past him on their way out and he stopped to watch them go. He recognized Bull Brody and Reno Marke, but did not know the others.

'Hold up,' Reno Marke said in a hoarse whisper as they reached the plankwalk. 'We can't go after the man now, not after the marshal's seen us.'

'Too bad,' Bull Brody growled, glancing back at the closing door. 'Because there he stands right now, and look who he's talking to.'

'Esperanza del Rio,' Marke said with growing irritation. 'Does that mean she hasn't gotten over it yet?'

'More likely,' another man whose name was Billy Short put in, 'she thinks she's found someone who'll listen to her fantasies about owning all of the land east of the Chickasaw and south of the Arapaho Range.'

'Well, it seems that she's found someone who will,' Bull said.

'Or is getting paid to,' Marke added. 'That man was quick to take a hand in there tonight.'

'Well, we can't get even with him tonight, not with the law right here. That's out. Maybe we ought to tell the boss that she's at it again and that she might have some help this time.'

'We'll do that; tell Mr Solon and then wait and see,' Bull Brody said 'Then, if we ever find Dancer on SS range, I don't care how many guns he's carrying, we'll take care of him.'

★ ★ ★

Tom Lang slowed the team of horses as they drew into the front yard of the small house. He could smell the river and hear a symphony of bass frogs, shrill cicadas and chirping crickets, all of which grew muted as the carriage carrying Tom and Dottie pulled up. The river, the Chickasaw, was only a quarter of a mile away from their twenty-five-acre holding. Here and there through the willow trees he could see star-gleam on the waters. His attention was on his house and the pole corral to the north. A group of curious colts had their heads over the top rail, looking at him. Thank God they were there. He had had a bad feeling about leaving them alone.

Those dozen shod horses and the land itself were practically his only assets. Helping Dottie down from the carriage, he tried to smile, knowing that she could see the worry in his eyes. Inside, Tom struck a match and lit the lantern bracketed to the wall beside the front door. Dottie hurried off to the bedroom to remove the boots she had worn all day on her job at Nichols' Store. He could tell it was getting harder on her by the day. Tom sagged into a leather chair and waited until Dottie reappeared in her night dress, her hair now unpinned to cascade in an auburn flow across her shoulders. She looked as young and fresh as ever.

She sat down in a chair facing Tom's

across the braided rug and low walnut table.

'What is it, Tom?' she asked, leaning forward to stretch her hand toward his.

'Same as always,' he replied. 'Solon is going to try to break through to the river again soon. Esteban Cruz tells me that they were bunching their cattle over near Sabine Canyon.'

'I see.'

'And, another thing, Dottie,' Tom said, hunching his body to lean closer to her. His eyes were intent, anxious. 'Suppose he resorts to other tricks to drive us off? Those dozen ponies — I finished putting shoes on the last one today. What if Solon were to drive them off? We'd be ruined. What if he decided to set fire to our house? I can't be here all the time, even if I could, I'd still be one man against Brian Solon's crew.'

'You worry too much, Tom,' Dottie said softly.

'Do I?' He was briefly thoughtful. He rose abruptly and let her hand drop. Pacing the room, he said, 'I think that

40

maybe I am worrying too much and not doing enough to fight back.'

'What do you mean?'

Tom had halted near the fireplace. Now Dottie rose to walk that way.

'Everyone is getting ready for a war but the small ranchers along the river. What can Esteban and I, the Everetts, the Suttons do alone? We're not soldiers, lawmen or gunfighters.' He paused and let his eyes linger on her pretty face for a moment.

'And Esperanza del Rio has now decided to play a hand again. I know,' he held up a hand, 'she makes quite wild claims, but she is determined. And she is ready to fight.'

'What do you mean, Tom?'

'You saw her tonight in conversation with that man who was wearing three pistols — his name is Dancer, I've been told. What is he doing here?'

'We'll never know,' Dottie answered.

'There's only one reason a man like that goes anywhere — to make trouble,' Tom, now overwrought, insisted.

'Maybe he just happened to meet Esperanza and they were just passing time.'

'In the street? At this time of night?' Tom shook his head. 'He's up to no good, and it is all concerned with the range war. What else could he have to talk to Esperanza del Rio about?' Tom asked sharply.

Dottie was smiling, and Tom frowned. 'What else could they find to talk about?' Dottie asked, 'A man and a pretty woman, I just couldn't guess!' she said, and as she spoke she rubbed the roundness of her belly where Tom's baby grew.

Tom was growing exasperated. 'We need help!' he said more loudly than he had intended. Still frowning he asked his wife, 'What about your brother, Jack?'

'You can't stand the sight of him, and I'm not that fond of Jack myself,' Dottie answered, returning to her chair.

'But he's a fighting man.'

'That's why they sent him to prison,' she reminded him.

'Maybe prison has changed him.'

'Does it ever?' Dottie asked.

'When is he being released?' Tom asked.

'I think he's already out. He probably went back to Singletree.' Which was the tiny foothill town where she and her brother had been raised.

'Dottie — let's send for him. We can't fight Solon alone. Remember the last time he drove one of his large herds through here? Every garden, crop, and half of the outbuildings were destroyed, our animals scattered.' He went on, 'You can't work in town much longer. If we lose the colts, we'll have nothing at all when the baby comes. We might have to move. I can't start over. I can't!'

Dottie knelt before her husband, resting her head on his lap. Despite the fact that Jack Doyle was her brother, she did not trust him a bit. He had lived with them briefly when they first came to Matchstick. He stole saloon money from her purse, drank most of the day and did nothing else but brag about the big day he had coming. Constantly fighting with men in town he had eventually been asked to leave. Jack Doyle was good with his fists, good with a gun and an absolute failure at everything else in life. Dottie lifted her eyes to the worried, bruised face of her husband.

'I'll send for Jack tomorrow,' she told him.

3

Dancer wasn't ready to rise when the sun began shining through his window, heating the small room he had taken at the Silver Palace hotel. The bed with its thin mattress and sagging springs was heaven after spending three nights in a row sleeping on the desert floor. And it had come with clean sheets! Dancer couldn't remember the last time he had slept between sheets. The room, on the east side of the hotel, was simply growing too hot and bright to sleep in.

So he rose without eagerness to face the day.

He slapped on his Stetson which had been sitting on a small, chipped bedside table and swung his legs to the floor. There was a water pitcher on the table as well, and two glasses. He poured himself a drink of water as he let his gaze wander over the room, searching for something that might have been changed overnight — an old habit.

Beyond the window there was a brief uproar and he walked across the room to lift the corner of one of the pale-blue curtains. Two passing teamsters had managed to lock the wheels of their wagons with each other in the middle of the street and were now busy yelling at each other instead of trying to resolve the situation.

Eventually the two came to some sort of agreement and with help from passers-by the wagons were pried apart and continued on their way. Dancer smiled thinly and opened the window to his room. He reflected how often men preferred to waste time arguing about their differences rather than discussing how to resolve them.

Dancer stepped into his black jeans and glanced out of the window again. There was a steady stream of traffic along the street, though the sun had barely risen. Matchstick, like all desert communities, conducted most of its business very early or quite late.

He looked at and sniffed his yellow silk shirt. It was one of his favorites, but it had seen some trail time. Looking into his bag, he pulled out a white linen shirt he had purchased in Mexico. By some magical process the shirt never seemed to wrinkle. It could be shaken out to look as fresh as the day he had bought it. He slipped into it and buttoned it up. He reached then for his holsters and took his third pistol from under the pillow. After tightening his belt, he started out to find a place to eat.

A few sets of eyes glanced his way as he crossed the hotel lobby, but Dancer was used to that. He had the feeling that word had gotten around Matchstick as to his identity and people were wondering what he was doing here.

Stepping out into the bright early morning sunshine Dancer looked up the street and down. He walked lazily away from the hotel, heading westward, mainly to keep the sun out of his eyes.

Within two blocks he began smelling welcome hints of frying ham and bacon, biscuits in the oven, freshly brewed coffee. The sign hanging from the beam of the covered plankwalk read: 'Sadie's.'

The restaurant was small but crowded with men and a few women. Dancer found a place to sit at the counter beside an elderly town man who glanced at Dancer, nodded and said ''Mornin',' before returning his concentration to his plate of food. A mug of coffee was slapped on the counter in front of Dancer before he had spoken to order it. He glanced up to see a young waitress with expressive green eyes, a broad mouth and a wealth of reddish hair.

'What'll you have?' she asked.

'Some of each,' Dancer replied. The girl smiled and walked away toward the kitchen. His order was not an uncommon one where hard-working cowhands, miners and teamsters built up man-sized appetites. Dancer looked around after the waitress had gone. A few men were staring at him, but their eyes shifted away as he returned their interested gazes. Theirs was only a natural curiosity about a stranger, especially one so well-armed. Dancer saw no one whose face he recognized, no one whose face indicated violent intentions.

'Another cup?' the girl asked. She had returned silently, and was refilling Dancer's coffee cup before he had a chance to answer. She smiled again. 'We're a little behind. One of our cooks didn't show up. It'll just be a few minutes more.'

Dancer nodded and the girl went away again, casting him a backward glance. She returned before Dancer had sipped his second cup halfway down. The platter she sat before him contained fried potatoes, ham, bacon, three fried eggs, hominy grits, biscuits and sausage.

'That ought to do the job,' Dancer said.

'You'd think so,' the girl said, poking

at her reddish hair with her fingers. 'Some of these hardworking men around here, especially the teamsters, ask for seconds.'

Dancer picked up a knife and fork. The girl had not yet left. 'You're the one, aren't you? I mean the one everyone is talking about.'

'I suppose so,' Dancer answered. 'Although I don't see myself as all that interesting.'

'You'd be surprised,' the waitress said. 'You interest me.'

There wasn't much to say to that, so Dancer began to eat. The waitress still stood there although a couple of men in the far corner were signaling to her. 'My name is Daphne,' she said, 'Daphne Smart.'

'Pleased to meet you,' Dancer said without offering his own name. She nodded and went to take care of other customers. Dancer worked away at his breakfast, but he was stuffed before he had gotten halfway through. He looked mournfully at his plate, regretting that he could not save the rest of the meal. What he ate along the trail was a pitiful excuse for food, and many times he had awakened on the desert with thoughts of just such a breakfast. Well, he considered, there could be too much of a good thing. He was fishing in his pockets for some change when Daphne returned.

'Everything all right?' she asked, looking at the half-empty platter.

'Fine. I guess my appetite has nothing on those teamsters.'

'It's a lot of food,' Daphne said, picking up the two silver dollars Dancer had left beside his plate. 'You did it justice. What are you going to do about supper? Or are you leaving town?'

Dancer frowned. 'I'm not leaving just yet. As for supper, I suppose I'll come back here. What's the special going to be?'

'It's not special,' she laughed. 'It's always the same, steak and potatoes.'

'Sounds good. I'll probably see you tonight then.'

'No you won't. I don't work nights. My father wouldn't like it,' Daphne told him. 'That's when the rough-necks, half-drunk, figure out that they should have something solid in their stomachs after a dozen or so whiskeys.'

'I see,' Dancer said. 'Then you usually cook supper at home, do you?'

'I do. And if you've nothing better to do, you can take this as an invitation.' She collected the platter, silverware and empty coffee cup and smiled brightly again. 'It's a small town — you can ask anybody where I live. Seven o'clock would be good.'

Before Dancer could answer, she swirled away and started off toward the kitchen again, leaving Dancer to ponder. Shrugging his thoughts away, he crossed the restaurant and went out into a morning which was clear, dusty and rapidly growing warm. He decided first of all to see to his horse, and started up the street toward the Come Along Stable, his thoughts returning again to the smiling Daphne Smart. He wondered . . .

* * *

'I want to know why that man was not arrested!' Brian Solon demanded. The bulky ranch owner stood in front of Marshal Peebles's desk, glaring at him. Peebles, as always, had his hair perfectly parted and pomaded. His mustache was neatly trimmed, his black shirt pressed, his nails trimmed. Did he spend all of his time at the barbershop? Of course: Peebles seemed to do little else from day to day. Solon figured the man had the time to spare.

'This man, Dancer, roughed up two of my riders in the Blue Ribbon last night as you perfectly well know.'

'Do I?' Peebles said, lifting his boots to his desktop, infuriating Solon who had already half-decided to have Peebles's badge. The man was not exactly obstinate; he was only inefficient when it came to carrying out Solon's suggestions. The marshal replied further:

'I went over to the Blue Ribbon last night after a disturbance was reported. I found two SS men who claimed they were roughed up.'

'Reno Marke and Bull Brody. I know. They told me.' Solon was having difficulty controlling his anger. His fleshy face had grown red.

'Bull Brody? Reno Marke? One man roughed them both up?' the marshal said. 'I would think it would take two or three men to rough up Brody himself.'

'That just shows you how dangerous this Dancer is,' Solon sputtered. 'Did you talk to him as I instructed you?'

'I talked to him yesterday at the hotel and again last night in front of the Blue Ribbon.'

'And found out nothing — like why he has come to Matchstick?'

'He didn't volunteer any information,' Peebles said.

'And you let it go at that?'

'What was I supposed to do, Mr Solon?'

'You should have . . . oh, I don't know. You're supposed to know how to handle these things, *Marshal*.' Mopping his perspiring forehead with his handkerchief, Solon paused for a minute. Then he said, 'I've heard that he was seen talking to Esperanza del Rio.'

'Yes, I saw them together,' Peebles said with a nod. 'And so . . . ? She's a beautiful woman. I don't find it unusual for a man to wish to talk to her.'

'Don't you see anything, Peebles? Esperanza and her constant complaint that I somehow stole her inheritance from her.' Solon made a disparaging sound. 'All nonsense, of course, but she continues to believe it. Personally I think the woman is mad. At any rate, here comes this known gunfighter into Matchstick of all places, and he falls into conversation with Esperanza del Rio.'

'Meaning what?' Peebles asked in his calm voice.

'Can't you see anything? She has obviously hired the man to do her fighting for her!'

'Esperanza?' Peebles seemed to consider this. 'She must be making more waiting tables than I thought possible — I don't think men like Dancer come cheap.'

'Maybe she had some family fortune hidden away, maybe she's promised Dancer a section of land. Maybe she's lured him in some other way,' Solon said with a meaningful, crooked smile.

'None of those seems real likely, Mr Solon,' the marshal responded. 'Do you mind if I ask you a question? Why don't you just buy those settlers out? Or drive your cattle around them?'

'Why should I?' Solon answered sharply. 'I have always used that stretch of the Chickasaw to water my steers when the water table was low. Always! There were no fences in this part of the country in those days.'

'There aren't any now,' Peebles said reasonably.

'There will be. Wait and see. Besides those puny little homesteads and dry crops are the same thing as fences. As to why I won't drive my herd around — the only decent trail is up the Cahuenga Pass toward Singletree. Can you imagine what it takes to drive six thousand head of steers up over that pass when they're already thirsty and balky. I'd run a lot of weight off them — if I could keep my whole crew together for that long. The men wouldn't stand for that rough ride when there's no reason for it. We've always driven the cattle straight through to the Chickasaw,' Solon said as if it were a God-given right.

'And,' he continued, 'until after I've sold off my year's gain, I don't have the money to buy the settlers off. There's some of them, like that damned Tom Lang and Esteban Cruz that wouldn't sell even at fair market price.' Solon's expression seemed to indicate that the small landholders were doing that just to spite him.

Solon put his hat on, preparatory to leaving. He paused long enough to bark, 'See that you control this man Dancer!'

Peebles rose from behind his desk and assured Solon, 'If I catch him breaking the law, he'll get locked up just like anyone else.'

That wasn't good enough for Solon, who continued to grumble under his breath as he stalked out of the marshal's office, slamming the door behind him.

* ★ *

'I can't see that it's anything you should worry about,' Agatha Wilkes said to her husband as she bustled around the small kitchen of their house. 'So you saw this stranger talking to Marshal Peebles? They could have been discussing a hundred things.'

Sanford Wilkes sat miserably at the kitchen table with its neat white tablecloth decorated with embroidered bluebirds. 'It was me, the bank; what else could it be?'

Agatha leaned against the sink with her arms crossed beneath her breasts. She was not an attractive woman with her overly-ambitious nose and small eyes, her receding chin and dull mousy hair. 'Well, if they're going to torment you over a few hundred dollars, why don't you just put it back?'

Sanford Wilkes smiled weakly. He had told his wife that he had borrowed a little cash from the bank to pay for her fancy carriage, but he had not admitted the full extent of his 'borrowing', nor had he told her that he had fallen deeply into a gambling habit while trying to win enough money to pay the bank back. If she understood the extent of his debt she would have good reason to worry. Sanford looked at his watch, replaced it in his vest and rose.

'I have to be going, dear,' he said and kissed the air in the vicinity of her cheek.

'Don't forget to go by the butcher's and pick up a pot roast on your way home. And don't forget my lace for the new curtains,' she said as she followed Sanford out on to the porch.

'I won't, dear,' Sanford said, swinging heavily into the saddle of his small gray horse.

Wilkes rode through the heat of morning toward the bank. He rode slowly, thinking deeply. There had to be some way out of this mess. In the back of his mind was the germ of an idea, but he would need an accomplice to pull it off, a man without fear. If something were not done soon, his career and his life in Matchstick would soon be ended.

Sanford Wilkes did not think that he would fare well in the Territorial Prison. If he failed, that was where he would end up. He had to find an accomplice, and quickly. The arrival of Dancer had started the clock ticking.

4

When Dancer returned to the Come Along Stable that evening it was with his saddle. His horse was looking rested and well fed, but it could use a little exercise. Porky Bing met Dancer at the stable door.

'Taking him out are you?' the stable hand asked.

'Just for a little while. I'll be bringing him back tonight,' Dancer answered, flipping his saddle blanket on to the horse's back and smoothing it. 'Just need to take a little ride.'

'Oh?' Porky Bing asked, hoping to receive a tidbit of gossip. The whole town was buzzing about Dancer. What was the man up to now?

Dancer swung his saddle up on the bay horse's back and adjusted it. Looking over the horse as he reached for the cinch, he asked Bing:

'You know a waitress named Daphne Smart who works over at Sadie's restaurant.'

'Not to talk to,' Bing said as Dancer tightened a cinch. 'But, I know her — everyone does.'

'Could you tell me where she lives?' Dancer asked. 'We've got a supper planned.'

'Daphne Smart?' Bing said with an expression of disbelief. He hadn't known Daphne to invite anyone to her house, ever.

'Something wrong with that?'

'No sir,' Bing said with a stammer as those cold gray eyes of Dancer met his. 'It's nothing to me. She lives out along Willow Street. Not much of a street, but that's what it's named. It's at the north end of town. Follow it out about half a mile east. On your right side you'll see a small white cabin with two sycamore trees in the yard — that's where she lives.'

'I guess I can find it,' Dancer said with a nod of thanks. He led the bay outside the stable before swinging aboard.

The sun was still hanging above the far mountains, glowing brightly, but its heat was beginning to dissipate and already in the east a single dully glowing star could be seen. It promised to be a pleasant evening. Finding his way after one false turn, Dancer rode to the front of the small whitewashed adobe house. Smoke rose in lazy curlicues from what had to be the kitchen stovepipe. The front door stood open, for ventilation he assumed, for though the sun had nearly set and the day was rapidly cooling, the small house would have trapped much heat throughout the day.

There was no hitch rail, so Dancer removed from his saddle-bags the set of hobbles that he always carried and fastened them on the forelegs of his horse. The horse looked offended, and even though Dancer knew that the horse usually stood for him, one never knew, and he did not want to lose the bay should a sudden sight or sound spook it.

Noticing a small circle of white painted-stones ringing a struggling flower patch, he stepped up on to the porch and rapped on the door frame.

'Come on in. I'm in the back,' Daphne called out, and Dancer did so.

The furnishings in the living room were sparse and plain. Above a native stone fireplace a mantel held several ceramic vases and assorted glassware. Dancer crossed the braided rug and entered the small, neat, white kitchen where Daphne, wearing a blue dress and white apron, stood fussing with something in the oven. It was still warm in there. Dancer asked:

'Can we have the back door open as well?'

'Please,' Daphne said, and Dancer swung the kitchen door open to the sundown-colored night.

Dancer seated himself at the small round table, his back toward the wall where he could see the front door and could not himself be seen through the narrow window in the room. Old habits die hard, but they had kept him alive this long.

'We won't be dining well, but there's plenty of it,' Daphne said, straightening to turn and face him. She smiled. Her reddish hair was pinned up artlessly and a few strands had fallen free. Dancer found the sight charming and he smiled in return as he studied her. Broad mouth, lips lightly rouged now, deep green eyes. She was slender and yet well-rounded where it mattered.

'Smells good,' Dancer said. 'What are we having?'

'Catfish and mustard greens. Plus cornbread — it's still baking; that's what's causing the heat in here.'

'Sounds fine to me,' said Dancer, who had often dined on poorer fare. 'Where is your father?' he asked, looking around.

'My father?' For a moment Daphne's eyes held an inexplicable, stunned expression.

'Yes,' Dancer answered. 'You told me

that your father wouldn't like you working nights.'

'I know I did. It's the truth, my father wouldn't like me working nights. Or wouldn't have,' she amended. 'My father's dead.'

'Sorry. What happened, if you don't mind talking about it,' Dancer asked, because Daphne's father couldn't have been that old when he died.

Daphne looked down, studying the floor. She held a long-handled wooden spoon in one hand. 'The land. The land killed him. That and his dreams,' she said slowly.

'Dreams can ruin a man,' Dancer agreed out of experience.

'More to the point,' she said, her eyes now hot and fixed, 'Brian Solon killed him by frustrating his dreams. Do you know who he is?'

'I've heard of him.'

'Father bought a section of land not far north of here, near a place called Sabine Canyon.'

Dancer only frowned. He didn't

know the area well enough to picture it. 'Well?' he coaxed as Daphne fell silent.

'Well, Brian Solon said that Father had no right to the land. He took Father to court to challenge the deed, his right to the land, and one of the crooked judges in Solon's employ agreed that Solon owned the land along the Sabine and always had. It was simply legal theft, leaving us with nothing at all.'

'It seems Solon can't have enough land to satisfy him,' Dancer said, although he was starting to feel uneasy about Daphne now. Was this why she had invited him here? To tell her story with hopes of enrolling Dancer's assistance? He remembered all too clearly his brief meeting with Esperanza del Rio. That was what the Spanish girl had had in mind, certainly. Daphne? Was that why she had taken an apparently immediate liking to him, invited him to her house for a meal?

Silently now she brought a huge platter containing a moderate-sized baked catfish and placed it on the table. There was no longer a smile in her eyes. She delivered smoking-hot mustard greens and returned to the oven where she used her apron as a hot pad, removing a tray with golden cornbread on it. This she cut into generous squares, stacking half of them on a plate. From the cooler she removed a tub of butter to be used on the greens and left to melt on the hot cornbread.

Daphne untied her apron and sat opposite Dancer. 'Eat,' she prompted, 'don't let it get cold.'

Dancer did so, almost greedily. It had been a long time since he had eaten a home-cooked meal, a long time since he had sat across the table from a pretty girl in the cool of evening. A long time since he had done many ordinary things, he reflected.

They ate in near-silence. When at last Dancer had finished, placing knife and fork on his empty plate, he scooted an inch or two from the table, thanked her for the meal and then felt compelled to speak.

'I'm very sorry about what happened to your father,' Dancer began, 'but . . . '

'But what?' Daphne asked. 'There's nothing to be done about it now, is there, Mr Dancer?'

'John,' he said without reluctance, studying the girl, looking deeply into her eyes. 'Please call me John.'

'All right,' she agreed with a fleeting smile. She now had her elbows propped on the table, hands clasped beneath her chin, studying him.

'There seem to be a lot of misconceptions about why I have come to Matchstick,' Dancer said.

'Why are you here?' she asked with apparent innocent interest. 'Of course, you don't owe me any explanation.'

'Maybe not, but I want to clear up any misunderstandings you might have about my purpose here.'

'Would you like to move to the living room?' Daphne asked.

'If you like.'

When settled into the stuffed chairs in the cozy room with the last glow of sunset for their lighting, Dancer began.

'I'm on my way to Scottsdale,' he told Daphne who watched with interested eyes, her hands clasped between her knees as she bent forward. 'But I can't arrive too soon. The man I'm looking for won't be arriving for another two days, and if I stay around in Scottsdale for that long, I'll be noticed and talked about just as I am here. That raises the chance that someone will find this man and warn him off.'

'Are you going to kill somebody?' Daphne asked with a small shudder. Dancer ignored her question and continued:

'So, I decided to stop off in some small town and wait a few days before going on to Scottsdale. I'm tired of desert riding, anyway, and my horse could use some rest and decent feed. I chose Matchstick only because it's on my way. I plan to stay here only so that my hand won't be tipped in Scottsdale and I lose the chance to get my man.'

'To arrest him?' Daphne asked, prodding hopefully. Again Dancer disdained to answer.

'I don't know who was the first to recognize me and spread the word around Matchstick, but it certainly spread, and everyone assumed I came here to help them or cause them trouble. I've had people ask me favors I have no intention of granting and others try to drive me out of town, which I won't tolerate. I suppose I'll go back into town, stable my horse up again and lie low in the hotel until it's time to travel on. Every town has its disputes and its share of petty squabbles, but Matchstick seems to have more than most. It's an unhealthy place, and I certainly can't do much to clean it up. Moreover, I don't have the time or the inclination to try.'

Daphne was nodding as if she understood, but she did not. She had been hoping to learn more about

Dancer: who, what he was. She knew no more than she had before he had confided in her. Suddenly she did understand one thing: the reason his jaw had tightened and his impenetrable eyes become more so at supper.

'You thought that's why I asked you out here for supper, didn't you?' She appeared offended. 'Because you thought I wanted to ask you for a favor — like the others — when I told you about my father and Brian Solon?'

'It crossed my mind, yes,' Dancer said. Daphne turned her eyes down briefly and then rose, raising her arms in a gesture of futility.

'Can't a woman just happen to like a man in your world, John?'

For a moment Dancer couldn't speak. He stood as well. 'It doesn't happen much, not to me. You have to admit it was kind of sudden, and with everything else going on around me . . .'

'Oh,' Daphne said in frustration,

adding a few words under her breath that he didn't catch. 'I met a man. I liked him. I thought I'd invite him to supper. That's it, can't you try to understand that?'

'I apologize,' Dancer said sincerely. Without planning it, he placed his hands on her waist, looked down at her. 'I'm so used to people doing things for selfish reasons, and Matchstick hasn't done anything to brighten my outlook on the human race. Until tonight,' he added, coaxing a small smile from Daphne.

Daphne seemed to blush. She glanced toward the window where the last color had nearly faded from the sky, blending into the darkness. Whatever she started to say next, she never got to it; she simply stepped away and smiled unconvincingly — her waitress's smile — and told him:

'I have to get to work early, John.'

'All right. Thank you for the meal, and for the conversation,' he said. Then he simply nodded and strode out toward his waiting horse. There was nothing left to say just then.

* * *

Mad Jack Doyle sat his horse in the yard of the small house on the outskirts of Singletree. He yelled once more and eventually a lantern was lit within. About time — Jack had been considering firing his rifle at the house a few times to rouse Carroll Gates. Gates who had been in the penitentiary with Jack was now staying with a frowzy former bar girl named Kate. Kate was the reason Jack had not gone up to the door. He couldn't stand looking at the sloppy, overweight blonde. Not in her nightdress, at least. How Gates could stand it, Jack couldn't figure.

Gates appeared on the porch just as Jack was thinking about reaching for his rifle to stir the household awake.

Gates held a lantern and stood peering into the darkness.

'Who is it!' he shouted. 'What the

hell you want, this time of night?'

'Get dressed, Carroll, we're riding!'

'Jack?' Gates asked uncertainly. After a minute his eyes adjusted enough to the darkness to make out Jack Doyle seated on his red roan. He hesitated, glanced back toward the interior of the house, and said, 'All right. Is there anything in it, Jack?'

'A little for sure, maybe plenty,' Jack answered. There was no sense in discussing it here — there would be plenty of time along the trail to Matchstick.

'I'll be out in a few minutes,' Gates promised, and he re-entered the house. Jack immediately heard a croaking, demanding female voice from within. He turned his head and spat. Gates had been locked up for a long time, but even so . . .

The little Mexican kid had found Jack in a saloon at six that evening and handed him a letter. Dottie was asking him to come down to Matchstick. There was some sort of trouble brewing

— she wasn't real specific about it. Already tired of Singletree, where he had spent the last of the few dollars they had given him upon release from prison, Jack Doyle knew it was time to be moving on; at least there was a chance of making some money. Besides, he really had no place else to go. And Dottie was a good cook. Tom Lang hated Jack's guts, but that didn't matter.

If nothing else, Jack told Carroll Gates as they started down the Cahuenga Pass, Tom had a small bunch of newly shod colts they could take if things didn't work out. But where there was trouble, there was usually a chance to make good money — if a man was willing to fight for it.

Jack Doyle was always ready for a fight.

No one called the stubby, swarthy man 'Mad Jack' to his face, but Doyle didn't mind having people across the territory referring to him in that way. The name carried a certain amount of menace with it, and cautioned men to treat him with respect.

The two men rode through the night with the rising moon lighting their way. Down the Cahuenga and across the grassland at the foot of Sabine Canyon, where they saw thousands of cattle and maybe a dozen cowhands riding night herd. Jake told Gates, 'We'd better ride clear of this bunch,' and Gates nodded his agreement.

Circling the herd, they therefore found themselves at the east end of Matchstick and not in the vicinity of Tom and Dottie's little homestead. The moon was still visible overhead, but it was whitening now as the fierce sun rose in the east. It would be hot in an hour or so. Already Matchstick was awake and moving in the mad rush to get things done before the desert heat built.

'You know this town, Jack?' Gates asked.

'As well as anyone, I guess. Why?'

'I'm thirsty, Jack,' Gates said, rubbing

his broad throat. 'There any saloons open yet?'

'Are you buying?' asked Jack, whose pockets were empty.

'I've got a few dollars,' Gates said. 'Unlike you, I've been eating my meals at home.'

Jack wondered who had paid more of a price for his meals, but said nothing about that, only answering: 'The Blue Ribbon is always open unless they've changed since I left here.'

★ ★ ★

Marshal Royce Peebles was just arriving at his office, the newspaper under his arm, when Porky Bing came running toward him, narrowly avoiding getting trampled by two cowboys who were racing their horses up the dusty street. They had a town ordinance against that, but even if Peebles kept a saddled horse in front, which he didn't, he would never catch up with the two wild racers.

Porky was panting, holding his chest as he arrived, gasping for air.

'Guess who I just saw?' Porky asked, his eyes wide and excited.

'I can't guess. Why don't you tell me?' Peebles said as he unlocked the door to his office and entered.

'Mad Jack Doyle, that's who! And he's got another mean-looking *hombre* with him.'

'Jack Doyle's back, is he? I thought they'd give him more time to serve than that.'

'Maybe he busted out,' Bing said, still in a state of excitement.

'Maybe. I can find out, though I never heard anything about it if he did.'

'I think they were headed to the Blue Ribbon, maybe you can walk over there and have a talk with them, find out what they're up to,' Porky Bing suggested.

'I might just do that,' Peebles said, though he had no intention of doing any such thing. He tossed his two-sheet newspaper on the desk and sat down.

'Thanks for telling me, Porky.'

'I'm always one to help out the law when I can.'

'I know that, and I appreciate it. You'd better be getting back to work now, hadn't you?'

'Yes, I guess so — I had only one other thing to tell you about.'

'Oh?' Peebles was getting a little tired of the stable hand. If Porky wanted his job, let him say so. Otherwise . . .

'The man they call Dancer. He came by last night and took his horse out.'

'Traveling on, was he?'

'No, he brung the horse back later, but before he left he asked me did I know where Daphne Smart lived. I reckon that's where he went.' Porky was still excited. 'That gives you something to think about, don't it?'

'That it does, Porky.' The marshal's eyes and inclined head motioned Bing toward the door. 'I'll see if I can find out what there is to that.'

And what was there to that? Peebles

wondered as Porky Bing left, closing the door on the hot sunlight outside. He knew, of course, as did everyone else in Matchstick, that Daphne Smart felt that her father had been legally cheated out of his 640 acres up along Sabine Canyon. So she had reason to hate Brian Solon, as did most everyone else in Matchstick. That didn't necessarily have anything to do with her meeting with Dancer. Yet it was soon after Dancer had met with Esperanza del Rio . . .

This man, Dancer, sure seemed to be stirring a lot of people up.

Maybe, Peebles thought, even though he was not a confrontational man by nature, it was his duty to find Dancer and ask him some hard questions this time.

And Mad Jack Doyle? Whatever his reason for being in Matchstick, his very presence promised trouble. Peebles snatched his newspaper from the desk top and unfolded it. He thought the editor of the paper might very soon have some splashy headlines that would increase his sales dramatically.

★ ★ ★

Jack Doyle and Carroll Gates strolled in through the green door of the Blue Ribbon saloon an hour later. Men glanced their way, looked at each other and a low murmuring buzz filled the rooms. Jack smiled inwardly. He was fond of attention and proud of his reputation as one of the territory's roughest men. Although he had actually only shot and killed two (or possibly three) men, his name was widely known and many unsolved killings were attributed to him. Jack reveled in it. Where a man like Dancer wished only for anonymity, Mad Jack Doyle craved notoriety.

Jack Doyle did not glance toward the gaming room, but if he had, he would have seen the banker, Sanford Wilkes, hovering worriedly over the spinning black-and-red roulette wheel. He held a small stack of silver dollars in his hand.

Wilkes had found that if he left the house a little earlier in the morning he had time to place a few bets on the devil's wheel before it was time to open the bank. The ball plunked into the twenty-six, popped out and settled on thirty. The croupier raked Wilkes's bet off the green felt. Almost wearily Wilkes glanced at his silver pocket watch. Was there time for two more spins, or even one? Porter Hall had a set of keys, too, and he could open up, but the teller was seemingly growing impatient with Wilkes's late arrivals, though he had never dared say anything about it. Sighing, his periodic optimism flattened again, Wilkes pocketed his money and started out, seeing a dozen men lined up along the bar, drinking the early hours away.

Wilkes used mentally to decry such men as lacking in all moral fiber or mental strength, but these days he was more tolerant. His habitual gambling had proven itself a compulsion every bit as strong as alcohol was with these men. In passing he noticed the two men sitting alone at a far table. He thought he recognized one of them . . .

Jack Doyle.

Although he had never had any business dealings with the man, he knew him as the one who waited for Dottie Lang on the wagon sometimes and once came into the bank with Tom Lang. His reputation was very low in this town. He was called a thief and a killer behind his back. Wilkes gave into sudden impulse and walked toward the table. He waited until he was asked and then sat down beside the other man, facing Jack Doyle.

'How's it going with you?' Wilkes asked.

'Little by little,' Jack answered. His dark eyes were probing. Why should the town banker want to sit down with him in a saloon?

'Do you have work?' Wilkes asked, hoping he wasn't being too nosy. He didn't want these two to get angry with him. Jack's answer, however, was moderate in tone.

'I figure to start helping my sister out again, for a while.'

'How much is she paying you?' Wilkes asked, unable to restrain himself now that he believed he had found his man.

'It hasn't been discussed yet,' Mad Jack Doyle replied, taking a sip of his whiskey.

'I have an offer I'd like you to consider,' Sanford Wilkes said in a very low voice. 'How would you like to make five thousand dollars?'

5

Royce Peebles decided it was time to go out and do some marshaling. Throwing his newspaper into the trash can beside his desk, he rose, carefully smoothed back his pomaded hair and planted his hat. Like it or not, he would have to ask Dancer a few tough questions. Pork Bing's revelations had brought Dancer back into the center of the complex politics of the local ranchers. Dancer certainly hadn't ridden to Matchstick on the chance of meeting women. There had to be a reason behind his presence here.

Or, Peebles considered, before bracing the man again, it might be wise first to interview Daphne Smart and see what she could tell him — if she was willing to talk. Peebles went out and tugged his hat low against the white glare of the sun. Then he traipsed uptown toward Sadie's restaurant, nodding to the people he met.

Looking in the restaurant window as he approached the door, Peebles saw Daphne standing at the end of the counter, talking to a man. Perhaps unsurprisingly, it was Dancer she was speaking with.

Well, Peebles thought, at least I don't have to go around looking for them. Each had a few questions to answer. Peebles settled his hat, shifting his gun, and entered the establishment, feeling just a little unsure of himself.

★ ★ ★

It was a simple enough plan, Sanford Wilkes was telling himself, and it should go off without a hitch. Simply, the bank was about to be robbed by two masked men. Wilkes was to hand over $5,000 to them and report to the auditors that $10,000 had been taken, eliminating any evidence of his own skimming of bank funds. Jack Doyle had leaped at the chance, though his partner seemed a little reluctant, as if he suspected a trap of some kind. Carroll Gates hadn't been out of prison long enough to forget its agonies. He didn't wish to endure them again.

'What about your sister, Jack?' Gates had asked.

'What about her? Think she has five thousand dollars? That can all wait a while — although her ranch might be a good place to hide out.'

'I don't like it,' Gates said, wagging his head heavily.

'Why not? It's a set-up. The banker isn't going to identify us. He has to watch his own back. Don't you see, it's practically a gift? He can never testify against us.'

Gates thought he had heard such talk before from Branch Tolliver, the last man he had robbed a bank with. That had gone horribly wrong, and Gates had found himself in the territorial prison afterwards. Not everything can be planned for, but he had to admit he couldn't find any holes in this simple scheme.

'All right,' Gates agreed with a sigh. 'Let's give it a try.'

* * *

Porter Hall was considering again a job opportunity he had been offered down in Phoenix. Matchstick was hot, isolated and dreary. This bank had been welcome as a start, but his view of the bank and its president, Sanford Wilkes, was rapidly paling. He glanced at the brass-bound clock on the wall. Wilkes was late, again. The banker was less than conscientious lately. The teller put on his eyeshade and went behind the counter. No one was in the bank this early. He occupied himself by counting money that didn't need to be counted. There were days when no one at all visited the bank for hours on end. This looked to be one of them. Hall yawned and then looked up sharply. He saw the flabby face of Sanford Wilkes at the front door. Two men he did not recognize were with him. New depositors?

When they entered, Porter Hall could see the pistols leveled on Wilkes's back. *A hold-up, damnit!*

Hall instinctively raised his own hands as the three men walked into the bank, one of them pausing to pull the shade down over the window.

'That's right, pal,' the short swarthy man said to Hall. 'Just keep those hands up. We don't want any trouble.' Then he barked at Wilkes, 'Where's the safe?'

'Back here,' Wilkes said. He was sweating profusely. His voice was thinned by fear.

'Let's see it,' the swarthy man ordered. To his partner, he said, 'Keep an eye on junior here.'

'He won't move,' the second robber promised.

Once in his office, Sanford Wilkes tried a conspiratorial smile. 'This should go smoothly.'

'So far, so good. Get that safe open.'

Wilkes nodded and got to his task. When the door to the safe was open Jack Doyle stared admiringly at the neat stacks of currency there. On the lowest shelf rested a box, which must have contained gold. Jack licked his lips. Wilkes removed a stack of currency and riffled through it.

'Five thousand, as we agreed,' he said with a fading smile, and handed the money to Mad Jack.

'I think I might need a little more,' Jack Doyle said and the banker recoiled. 'Find a sack for me,' Jack ordered.

'See here, now. Our agreement . . . ' Wilkes stuttered. Jack Doyle cocked his pistol.

'It was a bad agreement. I've changed the terms — now find a sack for the money!'

In the other room Porter Hall, his hands still raised, was studying Carroll Gates's face, causing Gates a little uneasiness. He had told Jack that they should wear masks, but Jack had said they were unnecessary. The bank teller had had long enough to look at him to notice every scar and mole on Gates's face. Gates had the feeling that he was in for a long ride to somewhere out of the territory. Even if no one in town knew his face, there were plenty of people in Arizona who did.

The banker and Jack emerged from the back room, the banker looking furious, Jack complacent. Jack Doyle still had the muzzle of his pistol jammed against Sanford Wilkes's back.

'Let's get going, Jack,' Gates said.

'What'd you have to use my name for?' Jack spat back.

'It don't matter — the teller there has been staring at me long enough to paint my portrait. Did you think of that?'

'Hell, it doesn't matter,' Jack Doyle said, then he pointed his Colt at Porter Hall and triggered off a shot that sent the young man reeling back against the wall, to slide to the floor.

'That wasn't a part of the deal!' Sanford Wilkes shouted, clawing at the still-smoking pistol in Jack's hand.

'Why don't you just shut up,' Jack said. He raised his gun hand and brought it down again, roughly, opening a deep red slash across the banker's forehead. Wilkes sagged to the floor.

'Did you kill him?' Gates asked.

'I didn't hit him that hard,' Jack growled, 'besides, what difference does it make? Let's get out of here — there's a back door in his office.'

*   *   *

Marshal Peebles entered the restaurant and started toward the end stool at the counter where Dancer was having a conversation with Daphne Smart, who was smiling prettily at him. In front of Dancer was a plate with a stack of hotcakes and bacon on it. There was a cup of coffee at his elbow.

At that moment from somewhere up the street a gun was fired. One shot only. Peebles glanced that way, but did not turn around. Someone was always discharging a firearm in Matchstick, which was against another town ordinance, but unless Peebles saw the man doing it, there was no point in investigating.

Instead he continued on toward the restaurant counter. Daphne Smart looked up, smiled at him; Dancer turned his head just enough to identify the approaching man.

'Coffee, Marshal?' Daphne asked.

'I guess I might as well,' Peebles said, taking the stool next to Dancer. 'I mostly came in to talk to Dancer . . . and to you.'

'It sounds serious,' Daphne said.

'I don't know if it is or not. That's the reason we have to talk,' Peebles said, removing his hat so that his pomaded hair glistened in the lamplight.

'What's this all about?' Dancer asked as Daphne went for coffee.

Before the marshal could answer, the door burst open and a wild-eyed man dressed in coveralls, wearing a straw hat, burst in and called out, 'Marshal, the bank's been robbed!'

'What are you talking about, Ernie,' Peebles asked, reaching for his hat again.

'I went in to make a deposit and found Wilkes on the floor, out cold and bleeding. As I went to see if I could help, I seen the teller. He'd been shot dead. The back door was open in Wilkes's office. I went there and looked out and seen two men hotfooting it away, carrying a bank bag.' All of this was related breathlessly. Peebles was already on his feet before Ernie had finished. He glanced at Dancer and rushed away, reaching for his pistol. Ernie followed, hoping for more excitement.

Daphne returned with a cup of coffee for the marshal, her face puzzled. 'Where did Royce go?'

'He just got word the bank's been robbed.'

'Why didn't you go with him?' Daphne asked.

'I've seen robbed banks before,'

Dancer said without expression.

'I mean . . . oh, well, do you want his coffee?'

Royce Peebles went first to the bank where a small crowd had gathered. A woman named Crissie Meredith was beside Sanford Wilkes on the floor of the bank, administering first aid. Peebles looked down in passing, glanced at the still form of the dead teller, and entered Wilkes's office. The safe door stood open. It was empty. At the back door he was able to pick out two sets of boot-prints going down the alley. They hadn't brought their horses with them, meaning that they were on their way now to retrieve them.

At a stable? Peebles went out into the alley as the doctor came in the front entrance of the bank to examine Wilkes.

Peebles broke into a trot. The boot-prints weren't hard to follow in the light dust. They seemed to be making their way directly toward the Come Along. As he ran through the heated alley, Peebles had time for conjecture. He knew that Mad Jack Doyle had come into town with a partner. Maybe Jack was not guilty, but he was sitting at the top of the marshal's list of suspects.

★ ★ ★

Leaving the restaurant after it became clear that the marshal would not be returning any time soon, and equally clear that his own presence was interfering with Daphne's work, Dancer heard the sharp report of two pistol shots. The patrons of the restaurant rushed toward the door, Daphne in their midst.

'What was that?' she asked fearfully, clutching Dancer's arm. Dancer shook his head. As the anxious crowd stood along the boardwalk in front of Sadie's, they saw two horsemen riding hell-for-it down the street and, a half a minute later, Marshal Peebles staggering out of the livery barn. He had obviously been shot, and hit badly. He looked after the escaping men for a moment and then swiveled on wobbly legs toward the restaurant. Dancer and Daphne rushed toward him, a few men following behind them.

Before they could reach Peebles, his knees had buckled and he fell to the dusty road. Dancer reached him first and turned him over. There were bullet holes in his chest, both high up, close together. Peebles squinted into the sun, managed to make out Dancer and started to speak.

'I saw the man to my left, couldn't see the other one in the shadows,' he managed to pant out. His voice was very weak; he was having trouble breathing, obviously.

'Who was it?' someone behind Dancer yelled. 'Was it the bank robbers?'

'I don't know who the first one was,' Peebles said in a near-whisper, coughing up blood. Now Dancer could see a little man with a medical bag running toward them from across the street.

Dancer propped up the marshal's head to try to keep his air passage clear.

'How bad is it?' someone called. Just then the doctor arrived and knelt beside Peebles with a mixture of trepidation and anger in his expression. Peebles opened his eyes and looked at Dancer.

'It was Mad Jack Doyle who shot me,' he said in an almost inaudible voice. 'Dancer,' he pleaded weakly, 'get him for me.'

'I'm not the man to do that,' Dancer answered in a gruff whisper. He wanted to reach Scottsdale the next day. There was a big payday involved. Dancer felt fingers tighten on his arm and glanced up to see Daphne, her eyes pleading.

'Please, John,' she said. 'There's no one else.'

Peebles managed to say no more. As the doctor worked on his wounds, Dancer rose, dusting off the knees of his jeans. Daphne still watched him with hopeful eyes. Dancer clenched his jaw and turned away from the gathered crowd. He strode up the street, Daphne following him with rapid little strides.

'John! Where are you going?' she asked with a touch of anguish in her voice.

'To the hotel to get my rifles, if I'm going hunting.'

Two or three people Dancer met as he walked back toward the stable, his two Henry repeating rifles under his arm, told him that Jack Doyle was likely to run to his sister's house up along the Chickasaw. They seemed eager that Doyle should be found, not so eager to chase after him themselves. A common theme. People loved to be on the very fringes of exciting events, none too willing to actually put themselves into one. You couldn't blame them; it's called the survival instinct.

Dancer's big bay horse was ready to go, eager to be on the trail again. After clearing the town limits, Dancer slowed his horse and began watching his surroundings more closely, studying the tracks in the dusty soil. His quarry had not slowed; they were not lying in ambush. Not yet.

Despite his reluctance to do the town's job for them, Dancer felt his spirits lift. This was when he felt most alive, the complete master of his fate. When his guns and tracking savvy were all that mattered. It was a life he was used to, and well suited to. He rode directly toward the river, having no knowledge of the area, with only vague directions to the Lang place, and that it was the destination of the bad men was based only on speculation.

Before he had reached the Chickasaw he had lost the trail of the bandits. He had expected as much. They had taken some sort of cut-off and were now riding directly to their hideout, whether it was the Lang place or another location. Hopefully they had paused now and then along the way, surveyed their back trail and decided no posse was chasing them. They would then slow their horses and, he hoped, become less alert.

It never did any good to guess at a

man's possible behavior. If you knew your man, that was one thing, but Dancer knew Mad Jack Doyle only by rumor, and rumors were not reliable. What sort of man he was, where he was going, how much of a fight he would put up if cornered were all unknown.

Along the river the air was still, rich with the scent of the willow trees that crowded its banks. The water ran thin and silver-bright. Blue-and-gold dragonflies skimmed the surface. Dancer rode once through a swarm of gnats, and ducked his head to avoid the curved trunks of sycamore trees which bent over the river as if studying their own reflections in the water. The water was the source of life here in the heart of the desert and quail were plentiful, and dove. He scattered a group of mule deer with his approach. The sun was warm, but not offensively so next to the river and a slight, pleasant breeze whispered through the willows and cooled him as he made his way northward between the river's sandy banks.

As he rode Dancer considered Daphne, her view of him, what she hoped for from him. She had been persistent in asking about his work. He hadn't known how to answer her, nor did he think that he would be around Matchstick long enough for it to matter. It was all very simple actually.

Dancer was a paid man. He went to great distances where the law could not follow. He was not a bounty hunter, for those people were paid by various government agencies for bringing in outlaws. Dancer was paid by individuals who had reason to want someone arrested but had no proof, an unwilling law officer, or reasons for keeping their thirst for justice a private matter.

So, yes, Dancer supposed he was what they called a hired gun, but he was discriminate in his work. Always paid in advance, he would try to track down a wandering son, a thieving former employee, a killer who had escaped the noose. He was not always successful, of course, but he always kept the money. Those who hired him were told that in the first place. But when someone had no one else to turn to, they came to Dancer and he would listen carefully to their troubles. If he honestly thought he could help, he would agree to take the job. If he did not, or suspected that his would-be employer might be lying to him only to purchase revenge against an enemy, these were shown the door immediately. Dancer had to live with himself, after all.

It was not an easy job to explain even to someone like Daphne who seemed to desperately want to know who and what Dancer was.

The river banks began to flatten and allow a view of the land beyond. It was long and mostly uninhabited, but Dancer was used to empty spaces. He had been a Texas Ranger for three years, and had ridden long and alone. The rangers, as most people didn't realize, usually had a force of no more than about 130 men. After having ceded much of its territory to the United States the Texas land still comprised something over 260,000 square miles. A lot for that many men to attempt to patrol.

Dancer was used to empty land and long traveling.

He began to spot occasional structures along the eastern shore of the Chickasaw and drew his bay up out of the river bottom to have a better look, hoping to find someone who knew where the Lang place could be found. He glanced at the sun. He could not miss arriving in Scottsdale in the next few days, and already this day was fading fast.

The bay struggled up the sandy bank, spraying white sand as it went. Directly in front of Dancer now was a small house, and before it three kids playing some sort of keep-away game with a long-haired mongrel dog.

They stopped playing as Dancer rode

slowly toward the house and stood gawking at him. They were Mexican kids, their dark hair straight, their wide eyes deep brown. Dancer drew up to talk to them, but before a word could be spoken, a Mexican man in his late twenties came around the corner of the house, a shotgun in his hands. He did not look happy.

'Are you from Solon?' Esteban Cruz demanded, eyeing Dancer's two rifles and the twin pistols riding on his hips.

'No, I'm not,' Dancer said quietly. 'I'm looking for the Lang place. Can you tell me how to find it?'

'Why you want it?' Cruz answered, squinting into the sun. His accent had deepened as his uneasiness grew. The kids were sent homeward with a gesture of his hand.

'I'm looking for a man who might have gone there — a man named Jack Doyle.'

'Mad Jack, he is back? No! He almost ruined Tom and Dottie when he was here last. He stole everything they had that could be stolen.'

'He's back,' Dancer assured him. 'They're saying that he robbed the bank in Matchstick and killed the teller.'

'Young Porter Hall? Oh no!' Cruz said, taking a moment to cross himself with his fingers. His expression hardened. 'Where is Marshal Peebles, then?'

'They gunned him down too — Mad Jack and his partner.'

'Oh no. He is alive?'

'It's kind of touch and go right now, I guess. Me, I'm what you might call a temporary deputy.'

Cruz continued to watch Dancer, his eyes dark, cautious and wary. He seemed to want to believe Dancer, understand his intentions, but he was being protective of his family and his friends.

'Do you wish to tell me where the Lang ranch is?' Dancer asked, his impatience now showing. 'If not, say so. I can find out from someone else, you know.'

'All right,' Cruz said at last. 'I will tell

you, but God help you if you are not who you say you are.' The man meant it.

Following Cruz's instructions, Dancer rode about two miles ahead and found himself on a low knoll overlooking a small house. Dusty live oak trees were scattered across the land; a couple of young colts frisked in a pen. Dancer saw no one moving about, but there were three horses, their heads hanging, tied to the hitch rail in front of the house.

They were there, then. At least, that was his strong assumption. All right, how best to approach this? Tom Gates and possibly his pregnant wife might be in the house. Dancer didn't want to start a shooting war under those conditions. Could he bluff his way in? Neither Jack Doyle nor his partner could ever have seen him. Still that seemed very risky. The situation called for patience. The two bank robbers would have to leave the house sooner or later. Dancer settled in for a long wait.

Sitting in the shade of a live oak tree, his horse munching grass beside him, Dancer studied the countryside. The river was silver-blue to the west, shallow but wide enough. The grass was generally pretty good, though mostly yellow this time of year. But there was no stock to be seen — unless you counted the dozen or so chickens scratching about in the Langs' yard. Reflecting, he realized that he had seen none at Esteban Cruz's little place either. Tom Lang had a small herd of colts held in a pen, but other large animals seemed to be absent from the land. He wondered how these small landholders were feeding themselves and their families.

Movement at the front of the Lang house brought Dancer's eyes back to the small house. Two men emerged, shielding their eyes from the sun with their hands. At this distance, Dancer could not make out their features. He didn't know what Jack Doyle and his accomplice looked like anyway.

The men looked as if they might be ready to move on. Each carried a bedroll toward his horse. Dancer couldn't let them get away now that he had found them. It was a dangerous tactic, but he decided to ride on down the slope. As he did so he saw the two men turn their heads toward him. There was a hurried conversation, then they went back into the house. Dancer kept going, riding slowly, easily — a man without a care in the world.

As he reached the flat, dry front yard he saw another man, this one wearing a red shirt, emerge from the house. He was not wearing a gun and he looked nervous.

'What do you want, stranger!' he called.

'Are you Tom Lang?'

'I am, but I asked you what you wanted.'

Dancer smiled and swung down near the porch, his eyes flickering to the front windows. He told Tom:

'I hear you got some shod young

colts you might be willing to sell.' Dancer glanced toward the pole corral and said, 'Oh, there they are,' and started that way, leading his horse, moving away from the windows. After a minute's hesitation, Tom hurried after him, his eyes narrow and puzzled.

'I'm up from Texas,' Dancer, told Tom. 'I work for the XO ranch.' An XO brand was in fact the one the bay horse wore, which was why Dancer had told him that. He knew that Tom would have already eyed the brand. Most Western men did.

'How did you hear I had those colts?' Tom asked. Dancer now stood with a boot on the lowest rail of the corral, watching the horses. One of them, a sleek little blue roan, approached him as he held out his hand to it.

'Well, I was passing through Matchstick and got to talking with a couple of men. I said if I could run across some young horses, I might be willing to buy them and take them back to my home range. Of course I'd need to hire somebody to help me along the trail . . . ' That was as far as Dancer got when Tom Lang suddenly stiffened and yelled out:

'Look out behind you! On the porch!'

Dancer ducked and spun. There was a man on the porch holding a pistol on him. He wasn't very good with it. As he fired, his bullet striking corral wood, startling the horses, Dancer fired back from his knee, his bullet striking the man in the chest, spinning him around. His knees buckled and he crumpled to the planks of the porch where he lay still.

Tom Lang stood frozen, his eyes as wide as those of the frightened animals. Dancer drew his left-side pistol as well, and with both revolvers in hand, started toward the porch. 'Who is he?' he called back across his shoulder.

'Carroll Gates is his name,' Tom said, now hurrying a little to catch up with Dancer.

'Where's the other one?' Dancer asked.

'You mean Jack Doyle?'

'That's who I mean,' Dancer said grimly.

'I thought he was in the house.' Tom clutched at Dancer's arm. 'Please, mister — don't go in there. My wife's in the house, and she's going to have a baby.' Lang's face was frantic now, ashen.

'All right,' Dancer agreed in a soft tone of voice. 'You go in. If Jack's in there, send him out.'

'What if he won't come?' Tom asked frantically.

'Then get to your wife and hold her to the floor. I'm not going away without Jack Doyle.'

Tom looked at Dancer's cold gray eyes, and knew that the man meant what he was saying. Tom stepped over Gates's body and went back to the front door, which remained open. Dancer moved around to the side of the house for cover.

He found himself almost face to face with Mad Jack Doyle.

6

Jack Doyle had a hungry look in his eyes. He was panting as if he'd run a mile. His Winchester was to his shoulder, its sights fixed on Dancer. When he spoke his voice was hoarse and harsh.

'Drop those weapons, mister. You might be good with your pistols but I've already drawn a bead on you and I guarantee I can pull this trigger before you can bring those guns into action.' Dancer's fingers opened and he let his twin Colts drop to the dusty earth, leaving him feeling half-naked.

'All right,' Dancer said. 'What do we do now?'

'I just want to get away,' Jack said. 'Will you let me, or do I have to kill you?' Dancer stood facing the man. The sun was hot, the breeze from the river intermittent. One of the colts in the pen nickered loudly. Dancer had started tucking in his shirt nervously with his thumbs. He started above his belt buckle and worked around toward the back.

'Are you alone?' Jack demanded, lowering his Winchester bare inches so that he was no longer sighting the rifle.

'Not quite,' Dancer replied as he drew his third revolver and swung it ground. He fired a fraction of a second before Mad Jack's rifle went off, the bullet digging a furrow in the white earth. Dancer's bullet was quicker and more accurate. Mad Jack opened his mouth wide in surprise. Blood was already rising to his lips. Then the bank robber, the killer, sat down hard on the bare earth and toppled over on to his side, quite dead.

A woman screamed behind Dancer as he was collecting his pistols. He jerked around to see Dottie Lang rushing toward them, half-restrained by her husband.

She glared at Dancer and screamed,

'You didn't have to kill him!'

Tom Lang's response was muted. 'Yes he did,' Tom said as Dottie hurried to bend over her fallen brother. He added almost to himself: 'It doesn't matter anyway. Jack would have been hanged sooner or later. He was just no good.'

Leaving the woman to sob over her brother, Dancer inclined his head and led Tom Lang aside. 'I'm sorry about this,' Dancer said.

'I can't see where you had any choice.'

'I didn't. She knows that too,' Dancer said, glancing toward Dottie, her face tear-stained and dusty. 'I imagine she's been grieving over Jack Doyle for years.' Dancer removed his hat, wiped at his perspiring forehead with his sleeve and went on. 'Now let's see about that money.'

'Money?' a dazed Dottie Lang said, joining them.

'They robbed the bank in Match-stick, took the money and killed the teller,' Dancer told her. 'That's why I'm here.'

'I sent for Jack,' Dottie told Dancer. 'I thought he had come to help me,' she said. 'Stolen bank money? I have no idea about that.' Her arm swept toward her house. 'Look for it if you like. Tear the place apart if you have to.'

It didn't come to that. Under the bed Jack had been given in the back room, Dancer found the leather-handled canvas sack with the bank's name stenciled on it.

'We could have used some of that,' Dottie said as she and Tom stood in the doorway, watching.

'Not of *that*,' Tom said. 'I can almost smell the blood on it.'

Dancer shouldered the bag and walked back to his horse escorted by Tom Lang. He tied the heavy sack on to his saddle horn. As he glanced up, his eyes met Tom's. 'Lang,' Dancer said, 'I've got a proposal I'd like you to listen to. It just might work out to your benefit.'

The town was quiet when John Dancer trailed back into Matchstick; it had an empty feel about it. Dancer was alone. Tom had agreed to take care of burying the dead men, and he planned on keeping their horses even though Dancer warned him that they were likely stolen. Tom had then ridden off to bring over a few of the local men — Cruz, Everett, Jim Sutton — and Dancer told them what he thought he could do to help them. No one argued with Dancer, but every man wore a dubious expression. At last Tom rose from his chair and said:

'If no one's got a better idea, I say we at least give it a chance.'

'All the same,' Jim Sutton said, 'I'm keeping my guns loaded and ready. Because Solon means to have his way.'

In Matchstick, Dancer noticed that the Blue Ribbon was busy, but it seemed less rambunctious than usual. He wondered if Royce Peebles had died

118

of his wounds. Saddle-weary now, Dancer made his way to the Come Along Stable and found it lighted. Porky Bing came forward to meet him. He asked:

'Have any luck?'

Dancer just shook his head. He was not ready to tell his tale just yet. He removed his two Henry rifles from their scabbards, untied the money bag from the pommel, and left Porky to strip the horse of saddle and bridle, to feed and water it. He walked quickly across the street, rifles under one arm, the heavy sack in the other hand. Thankfully he ran into no one who recognized him. Dancer was not in a talkative mood.

He crossed the lobby of the Silver Palace hotel, hearing only a few murmured words being exchanged behind him, and mounted the stairs. His boots made little sound along the carpeted corridor. He saw no one upstairs, heard no voices.

He stopped short as he reached his room. A narrow ribbon of light was seeping under the door. Someone was inside — Dancer certainly had not left a lamp on all day. He took a slow breath, palmed his right-hand Colt and leaned his shoulder against the door. It thwacked open and he came face to face . . .

With Daphne Smart, who was sitting cross-legged on his bed, wearing jeans and a red flannel shirt. Her eyes went wide as she saw the revolver in his hand. Dancer holstered the pistol and leaned his rifles against the wall in the corner of the room. His tone was gruff when he asked:

'Do you mind telling me what you're doing here?' He dropped the money bag on to the floor.

'I've been waiting for you,' the redheaded girl said in a small voice. 'I wanted to make sure you got back all right.'

She stood then and ran uncertain fingers through her hair, looking slightly embarrassed.

'I'm all right,' Dancer grumbled,

winging his hat toward the bedside table. Then he noticed his yellow silk shirt. Washed and pressed, it sat over the back of the wooden hotel chair. 'Why'd you do that?' he asked Daphne.

'It needed cleaning, and I had to keep busy.'

'Why?'

'I got to feel like I was waiting for a soldier to come home from the war — and I was the one who sent him.'

'No one sent me,' Dancer said, still cross.

'No, I know, but I sort of . . . John, are you all right?'

'Fine. Just tired and hungry.'

'Do you want to come out to my place and have something to eat?' she offered.

He lifted his hard gray eyes, half-smiled and said, 'I don't want to get off this bed, but thanks. How's Peebles?'

'He's still alive. The doctor said one of the bullets went right through the marshal. The other one hit a bone and shattered. A fragment went into Royce's throat near . . . something to do with talking . . . ' she looked uncertain.

'His larynx?' Dancer provided.

'Yes, that was the word the doctor used. He seemed more concerned about that than the damage done to his chest. Royce had his throat wrapped with gauze. He was ordered not to try to speak for a few days.'

Dancer had unbuckled his gun belt and placed it on the table. Now he stowed his third pistol, as usual, beneath his pillow. He looked up at Daphne who stood there, hands clasped together. She looked very young and fragile.

'Maybe you should have stayed with Peebles instead of coming up here. He'll be needing some care.'

'Oh, he has company, a nurse,' Daphne said, smiling for the first time since Dancer had rushed into the room holding a gun.

'Who?'

'You wouldn't guess — Esperanza del Rio.'

'That one?' Dancer nodded his surprise. He began pulling off his boots. Daphne watched him for a moment.

'You were serious about turning in this early.'

'I was,' Dancer replied. 'I rode quite a long way today and I've got a long way to go tomorrow.'

'To Scottsdale?' she asked with ill-concealed disappointment.

'No. I suppose that business can wait another day. I've got to have a talk with Wilkes when the bank opens. Then I'm going to pay a visit to Brian Solon.'

'Solon? Dancer, please think it over.'

'I already have. Goodnight, Daphne. Blow out the lamp on your way out, will you?'

$\star$ $\star$ $\star$

Dancer slept fairly well. He never let yesterday's trouble linger, and there was no point at all in thinking of the troubles a new day might bring.

The bank was not open yet. The

123

eastern sky still held dawn colors. He carried a blanket in his arms, wrapped around some bulky object. No one paid any attention to the bundle. He wasn't going to carry the bank bag around for everyone to see, and he certainly wasn't just going to tuck it under his bed, so he had wrapped it in his striped blanket and tied it up. It was awkward to carry and heavier than it might have appeared.

Should he have breakfast while he waited for Wilkes to open the bank? There was little else to do, he decided, so he started toward Sadie's restaurant. Daphne was there, looking bright and cheerful, but when he took a seat at the familiar end stool at the counter, she seemed to avert her eyes. Dancer placed his bundle at his feet and waited until she arrived with a coffee pot and cup.

'What's the trouble?' he asked quietly. She looked down and shook her head. When she looked up again, Dancer could see that her eyes were moist.

'Tell me,' he coaxed.

'I don't like what you plan on doing today,' she said in an unsteady voice. 'You might get yourself killed.'

'I'm doing it to keep a lot of other people from possibly getting killed,' Dancer told her.

'That all sounds so very noble, John,' Daphne said, 'but what about . . . ?' From across the room two men were calling for a waitress. Daphne started away. Dancer took her wrist, but she shook his hand off and walked away, crossing the restaurant to greet the two waiting men.

Dancer drank his coffee and ordered a breakfast which he dawdled over but Daphne did not approach him again until it was time for him to leave. Neither one of them, it seemed, really felt like opening the discussion again.

Paying, Dancer watched the girl's face for a long time, but she would not look at him, so he shouldered his bulky bundle and went out into the sunshine once more, feeling defeated.

He passed the bank which was still closed and continued on his way. He felt obligated to pay Marshal Peebles a visit, so he crossed the street again and went into the doctor's office, which was quiet, smelling of antiseptics. No one was in the office, neither patient nor physician, so Dancer passed through and made his way down the hall past rooms intended for the ill or wounded who needed hospitalization.

Peebles was in the second room on the right. Sunshine shone through the thin yellow curtains on his bedroom window, but most of the room was still in darkness. Royce Peebles, awake or asleep — Dancer could not tell which immediately — sat propped up on his bed, his throat bandaged, his normally neat pomaded hair sticking up at odd angles from his scalp, which seemed small, misshapen without its usual slicked-down covering. As the marshal shifted in bed, his blanket slid down a few inches and Dancer could see that his chest was also heavily bandaged.

There were dark crescents under each eye and he was unshaven. Dancer placed his bundle down beside one of the two empty chairs next to the bed. Peebles's eyes flickered open.

'Hello, Peebles,' Dancer said as he seated himself in one the chair.

'No!' Esperanza del Rio swept into the room, wearing black from head to toe. 'You must not have him talk, Dancer. The doctor says he must not yet.'

'I wasn't trying to make him talk,' Dancer said apologetically, though he realized belatedly that Peebles might have tried an instinctive response to his greeting.

'He must say nothing, not if he is to get his throat well,' Esperanza said, removing the black lace mantilla she had been wearing, letting it drop to her shoulders. Her hair was pinned up, glossy and perfumed with a Spanish comb holding it in place.

'I just came to tell him a few things that might make him less worried,'

Dancer said, looking at Esperanza and not at the silent Peebles. 'I got the two men who shot him.'

Peebles waved an excited hand, and Dancer guessed his meaning. 'One of them was Mad Jack Doyle. The other never introduced himself.' Peebles looked pleased. Esperanza placed a white hand on his forehead.

'Also I have the bank's money. I'm taking it over to Wilkes as soon as he opens up.'

Peebles's lips started to move. 'He says thank you,' Esperanza told Dancer. Obviously the Spanish girl had taken over as a full-time nurse.

'Are you spending much time here, Esperanza?'

'Every minute that I can,' she answered. 'He cannot talk, but that is all right. I talk — enough for both of us, and even when he is sleeping, I talk to him. About many things.'

Dancer figured that included continuing to pester Peebles with complaints about Brian Solon's expropriation of her land grant property, but he said nothing.

'I'm going out to pay a visit to Solon today,' Dancer said. 'I might have found a way to prevent a range war with the settlers along the Chickasaw.'

Peebles's eyes showed interest, but since he could not speak, Esperanza took the opportunity to butt in. 'I will tell you how to solve the problem with Solon: make him give me back my land and chase him and his cows away!'

Dancer only shook his head. Peebles, despite the pain he was feeling and the audacity of the woman, managed a smile. As if he were proud of her.

'The doctor says he needs this room to use,' Esperanza told Dancer. 'And so I went out to find two men to help me move the marshal to my house. He will stay there with me until he is well. I will continue to nurse him.'

Dancer continued to wear a fixed expression, but he wondered if all this was leading somewhere in Esperanza's mind — and in the mind of Royce

Peebles. Dancer rose from his chair and shook Peebles's hand. When he released it, the marshal began gesturing to Esperanza who somehow, practice perhaps, managed to understand his meaning. She went to the small closet on the opposite wall and riffled through the clothing hanging there.

She returned and handed a small object to Peebles. When he opened his hand the town marshal's badge gleamed brightly in the morning sunlight.

'He wants you to put it on, take his place until he is well,' Esperanza said.

'I'll be riding out soon. I have an appointment in Scottsdale,' Dancer told her and Peebles, who frowned slightly. He gestured and held up one finger.

'The marshal says just for today, wear it just for today — it might give you some protection against Brian Solon.'

Dancer doubted that, from all he had heard about Solon, but he took the badge, nodded his thanks and pinned it to the front of his yellow silk shirt.

Since Peebles was incapable of administering an oath, that was that, and after saying his goodbyes, Deputy Marshal John Dancer walked out of the doctor's office, and started on his way toward the bank, feeling the weight of the badge even more than that of the stolen gold in the bundle he carried.

The door to the bank stood open and Dancer pushed on through it into the interior of the building. Sanford Wilkes sat at his desk in the rear office, and he looked around with startled eyes. There was a bandage on his head still, and he was sweating freely although the day was not yet hot. His eyes went to the badge Dancer was wearing, but he made no comment.

'Yes?' the banker asked nervously.

'I have something that belongs to you,' Dancer said, taking the bundle from his shoulder. He untied and unwrapped the blanket and lifted the bank bag from its concealment. Wilkes rose from his chair in surprise and stood over the bag, his eyes widened to near roundness. He babbled at Dancer.

'Where did you . . . how did you?'

'That's not important for you to know,' Dancer said, crouching, his hat tilted back on his head. He lifted the heavy sack and placed it on Wilkes's desk. It thudded and jingled as it settled. 'What is important is that you count it and make sure it's all there.'

'Of course, I see,' Wilkes sputtered. 'It will take awhile. With my teller . . . gone.'

'Take care of this first. I'll stand out front and tell people you'll be closed for a while,' Dancer replied.

'Yes. Yes, of course,' Wilkes agreed without hesitation. 'You don't need to watch me, though.'

'I don't intend to. I just want to stay around long enough to see the safe door locked behind the loot,' Dancer said. Wilkes was an odd combination of emotions just then. He was eager, yet wary. One moment his eyes glittered, the next his mouth was drawn mournfully down. Dancer figured that the banker was thrilled to have the money back, fearful that some would come up missing. He left Wilkes to his work — there was nothing interesting about watching someone total up numbers. Dancer walked to the front door and started to close it just as a farmer in overalls and a straw hat — the one who had first reported the robbery — approached the bank.

'Not open yet,' Dancer told him.

The farmer pulled up short. He had a small leather purse in his hand. 'It seems this bank don't want my business,' he complained.

'Go get yourself a cup of coffee and come back,' Dancer directed. 'The banker's tied up just now. It won't be long.'

The farmer — Dancer now remembered Peebles calling him Ernie — muttered a few choice words and ambled off toward Sadie's restaurant.

Dancer returned to stand in the doorway to Wilkes's office. The little man was intent on his work. Banded stacks of bills were counted and placed aside. Wilkes kept tally, talking to himself under his breath. His expression didn't show it, but inside Sanford Wilkes was rejoicing. He was free at last of any possible suspicion. The bank robbers had to be dead, or else Dancer wouldn't have the recovered money.

Wilkes vowed to himself that this was the end of his gambling and the end of Agatha's free-spending. They would live within their means and make the best of it.

Dancer continued to watch the banker as he placed the sheaves of currency into the safe, replaced the stacks of gold coins and closed the steel door firmly, locking it down. Wilkes stood, mopping his perspiring forehead with a handkerchief. His face was florid, his eyes bright.

'We're short,' he told Dancer. 'About five thousand dollars short.'

Dancer wondered briefly whether Mad Jack Doyle had given some of the loot to his sister, but there was no way of knowing, and besides it was not his affair any longer. Wilkes was still speaking.

'I expect we can absorb the loss, though I don't like the idea of its being missing.'

Dancer said, 'All we need to know is whether you're going to hold the town accountable for the loss.'

'The town?' Wilkes looked sincerely perplexed. 'Of course not. Why should I? Because Marshal Peebles couldn't be in the bank to halt the robbery? You've brought back the bulk of the money, Dancer. For that I give thanks; for the lost money,' he gave a small shrug, 'I consider it a hard lesson learned.'

7

There was a clump of a dozen or so pine trees on the knoll, the first Dancer had seen anywhere in Cameron County. There were twice that many crows perched in the high, dusty branches of the trees and these took to wing, shouting hoarse bird curses back as Dancer guided his bay horse through the pines. Beyond the trees he could see the white, two-storied house that was Brian Solon's home. It was of plastered adobe. A red-tile roof, slightly pitched, sheltered it from the weather.

Dancer thought inconsequentially of the way those red tiles had been formed. They had to be tapered to overlap and form a seal against rain. The early settlers had come up with an ingenious method of manufacturing. Indian and Mexican women used their bare thighs as forms for the red clay tiles. He doubted it was still done that way.

Beyond the broad valley he caught a glimpse of what had to be the Cahuenga Pass trail snaking up the flank of the dust-colored hills there, toward the settlement of Singletree. He could understand why Brian Solon was not eager to try to drive 6,000 cattle up and over that rise to water at the Chickasaw.

Maybe he wouldn't have to — if the man was willing to bargain.

The bay horse seemed to drag its way down the long trail toward the flats below as if it were wary of crossing SS land. That might have been Dancer's imagination, of course, but he himself was riding cautiously. He was no friend of Brian Solon, and his inherited marshal's badge provided only limited protection on this ranch which, like many large spreads in the south-west, was considered by its owner to be an independent fiefdom with its own laws, immune from outside interference.

Local law was unlikely to try to enforce its own strictures against a landowner who commanded fifty or a hundred riders, who was likely to be prominent in local politics and whose operation was usually the town's largest source of income.

Crossing the ranch yard where a dozen live oak trees grew in a scattered rank, Dancer noticed that there were very few men around. That made sense if they were out tending to the large gathered herd. He did pass one man standing near the stable, pitchfork in hand, another methodically but with little apparent eagerness chopping wood near the wood pile. Behind the house he saw a man on the porch of one of the two bunkhouses, sitting in a chair, a crutch propped up beside him. All of the men studied Dancer with interest as he made his way to the front of the ranch house, swung down and tied his horse to the hitch rail.

Walking up the steps to the big oaken double doors, Dancer paused, looked around once again and rapped his knuckles on the door. A long minute later the door was opened by an old man with a crown of spiky hair circling his bald head. His nose was overlarge, his posture hunched. He studied Dancer with dark suspicion.

'What is it?' the old man croaked.

'I'd like to see Mr Solon.'

'Who's calling?'

'Tell him the marshal would like a few words with him.' Dancer indicated the badge he wore, tapping it with one finger.

'I'll see if Mr Solon will talk to you,' the little man said. He left the door open as he turned and started away into the interior of the house. Dancer stood there, looking at the dark wood of a staircase leading upstairs, the row of trophies on the wall over the large fireplace: elk, bear, cougar heads. There was an oversized Indian-weave blanket on the polished wood floor, several smaller ones hanging on the white walls.

A shuffling of feet announced the return of the wizened old man who was a full foot shorter than Dancer.

'He says he'll talk to you,' the man said. 'If you'll follow me.'

Dancer was escorted through an arched passageway into the cool interior of the big house. At the end of the corridor a heavy oak door stood open to a room. The old man pointed that way and reversed his direction, leaving Dancer alone in the hall. Dancer strode toward the room, boot-heels clicking on the flagstone floor.

Entering, he found Brian Solon behind a broad desk shuffling through some papers. The room was lighted well by an arched window set in the opposite wall. One other wall was composed of bookshelves well stocked with varieties of books in leather bindings.

'My wife used to read a lot,' Solon said, as if it were the first question everyone entering the room asked. His tone was proud and disparaging at once. Dancer thought he meant that it was fine for a woman to read. Not that he would ever waste his own valuable time doing it. Only now did Solon seem to recognize his visitor.

'When Hogan said the marshal was here. I assumed it was Royce Peebles. What are you doing here?

'Peebles won't be traveling for a while.'

'Oh, yes, the bank robbery. I heard about that. That certainly can't be the reason you're here.'

Solon, heavily jowled, dark-eyed, wore a wrinkled blue shirt and unbuttoned vest. His expression was not malignant, but set, as if prepared to be angry.

'No, it's not that,' Dancer assured him.

'And what gives you the right to go around calling yourself a marshal?' Solon asked.

'Peebles deputized me — temporarily.'

'That's not a deputy's badge you're wearing.'

'No. It's the only one that was available at the hospital. It's Peebles's badge. I'm acting marshal until Peebles can return to his duties.'

'Who says?' Solon asked with a scowl. 'Did anyone consult the town council?'

'No. Does he need to do that to appoint an acting marshal?'

'I don't know,' Solon grumbled, 'but I intend to find out. No one even knows who the hell you are.'

Dancer didn't respond. An apparently habitual belligerence seemed to be building up in Brian Solon. The rancher had another idea.

'If this is about that ruckus in the Blue Ribbon, when you roughed up two of my men . . .'

'That's not exactly what happened,' Dancer told Solon. He glanced at a nearby chair and let his eyes question Solon. With his own eyes Solon directed Dancer to the chair. Dancer sat and fixed his gaze on Solon.

'Those men of yours were in the

saloon, drinking — a little too much, it seems,' he said. 'One of them kept making a play for a bar girl, thinking she liked him. She didn't. Your man, I think Reno Marke is his name, started grabbing at the girl and shoving her around. As deputy marshal I couldn't let that sort of thing go on.'

'You weren't a deputy then,' Solon growled.

'I hadn't a badge yet,' Dancer said, 'but I was a deputy. Royce Peebles had sent for me to help him out.'

'To help him with what? I haven't seen Peebles out trying to help himself much. All he seems to do is get barbered — on town money.'

'I'll get to that in a while,' Dancer said. 'I'm just telling you that Peebles wanted me for his deputy.'

'So that's it,' Solon said with a movement of his mouth that might have been a smile. 'The word was that you were here to work for Esperanza del Rio.'

'I've heard that. There were a lot of

people with different ideas as to why I came to Matchstick. None of them was even close to the truth. I never had any contact with Esperanza del Rio. I only met her because of the bar fight. She was the girl Reno Marke was molesting.'

'Why, the damn fool!' Solon exploded. 'Of all the women in this town, he has to annoy her. She's crazy, you know?'

'Possibly. I tried to talk to your men, but they weren't listening. When Marke came after me, and later the other man, the big one . . . '

'Bull Brody,' Solon provided.

'Bull Brody, I had no choice but to fight them.'

'The boys tell me it was pretty dirty fighting,' Solon said, resuming his sulking scowl.

'I suppose it was. But I wasn't going to stand there and trade punches with a man the size of Bull Brody. Actually the boys got off pretty easy. I could have locked them both up for the night.' Which was untrue, but seemed to soften Solon's expression a little.

'All right,' the ranch owner said, leaning forward to rest his forearms on his desk, his eyes as hard as ever. 'Then suppose you tell me exactly why you are here, *Marshal* Dancer.'

Dancer said, 'It's about watering your stock along the Chickasaw. Running your cattle through and over the homesteaders' property.'

'That's what I have always done — before a single one of those scratch-dirt farmers had raised his shack over there.'

'That was a different time, Mr Solon,' Dancer said.

'So you're siding with them, are you?' Solon asked angrily.

'No, sir. It's the law I'm concerned with. You have no right to run cattle over those people's struggling crops, raising dust, scaring hell out of their animals and children. I know that the Cahuenga Pass road is tough and treacherous and you have no wish to try pushing six thousand head of cattle up and over it.'

145

'Damn right I don't,' Solon said through clenched teeth. 'I could lose hundreds of cattle along the way. Lost, strayed or stolen.'

'That's why I am here to talk to you, the reason I've talked to the settlers along the river.'

'From what I hear they're getting ready to string wire, to force a shooting war.'

'I've persuaded them to hold off on stringing wire.'

'Which side are you on, exactly, Dancer?'

'The side of logic, I hope. Tell me, Solon,' Dancer said, apparently shifting topics, 'have you ever driven a trail herd through Indian country?'

Solon's forehead furrowed. His eyes blazed. 'Of course I have. We used to follow the Goodnight-Loving trail up from Texas to the Kansas trailheads. We crossed Indian land all the time.'

'And how did you manage to get through — without starting a war?'

'I don't know what you mean. We

paid a grass tax, as we used to call it. Let the Indians cut out a certain agreed-upon number of beeves from the herd. There were already few buffalo roaming that land by then. They were glad to get the meat; we were glad to have the graze and water. What has that to do with anything?' Solon asked.

'Just this,' Dancer said, leaning forward to level his gaze on Solon's dark eyes. 'Those people along the Chickasaw are beef poor. I've been on their ranches. I don't know how they feed their children. You were once willing to work out a fair tax with the Indians. Why can't you work out something equitable with the settlers? If they let you use a certain corridor to reach the river, why can't you let them have a few cattle every time you need to reach the Chickasaw?' Dancer held up his hand as Solon immediately began to object to the plan.

Dancer went on. 'If you drive the herd up the Cahuenga, you yourself said that you might lose hundreds of cattle. If you choose to drive through to the river from where you now have them gathered, the settlers will fight. You will lose some cowhands, certainly. Maybe some of your best men, men you can't easily replace.'

'If the settlers are wiped out I have no more problems,' Solon said.

'Sooner or later the territorial governor would hear of it, and you'd see marshals from Phoenix in here, maybe even the Arizona Rangers — then you will have a fight on your hands and criminal charges laid on you. Why, Mr Solon? When it could all be so easily solved?'

'They'd try to skin me in any dealings,' Solon grumbled.

'Probably, and you'd try to skin them. Talk with their leaders, compromise and come to a fair bargain. Any other way and you lose.'

'I don't — '

'Will you think about it?' Dancer asked.

'I don't . . . I'll think it over,' Solon

said looking somehow dismal, relieved and combative all at the same time. This was a complicated man, Dancer decided. He could only hope that pragmatism would carry the day. Dancer rose from his chair and settled his hat on his head. Solon did not rise. As Dancer reached the door he did hear Solon grumble:

'What kind of lawman are you, anyway?'

The answer was that Dancer was no kind of lawman. He didn't wish to be one. He had done all he could for the people of Matchstick and its environs. It was time to be riding, before the Scottsdale project evaporated in the desert heat. Surely Royce Peebles knew someone else he could deputize to keep the peace in town?

Dancer crossed the porch as another man was coming up the steps. Dancer recognized him — his name was Short. He had been with Reno Marke and Bull Brody that night in the Blue Ribbon saloon.

Billy Short kept his eyes turned down, as if he did not recognize Dancer.

He watched as Dancer walked to his bay horse, checked the cinches and swung into leather. Now what do you suppose Dancer was doing here on the ranch? Talking to the boss, no doubt. About the incident at the Blue Ribbon, of course — it had to be.

Billy Short stood frowning into the bright sunlight, watching Dancer ride away. Billy thought that he should have guessed that the trouble over that event was not at an end. He, Reno Marke and Bull Brody had not exactly told Solon the whole truth about what had happened in Matchstick that night. So Dancer had come out to the SS to bring it all up again, possibly to embellish it. Why would he do that? Something was in the works, that was for sure. Of course Billy and everyone else on the SS knew that Dancer was working for Esperanza del Rio. Was Dancer trying to use the fracas at the

Blue Ribbon to influence Brian Solon in some way? How?

Billy couldn't guess, but Dancer's presence on the ranch could not bode well for the three of them. He had to warn Bull and Reno. Because Dancer was certainly up to something even if Billy Short couldn't guess what it was.

Now was the time to stop Dancer, while he was on SS land. Where he could expect no witnesses and no help. Billy Short returned to his hitched gray horse and swung into the saddle. He knew where Reno and Bull could be found, and Reno, at least, had sworn to fight the man the next time their paths crossed.

Well, now was the time. If something happened to Dancer on the open range, it might even never be discovered.

★ ★ ★

The sun was hot, the breeze dry. At this distance the Chickasaw had no cooling effect. The bay's hoofs were dragging, kicking up puffs of dust, and Dancer let the horse pick its own pace. There was no point in racing on in this heat. Not when he had no real place to go. Back to Matchstick, certainly, but the town would still be there when he reached it. He would need his horse to be fresh when they began the long ride to Scottsdale, unless he traded it for another, which he did not intend to do. That meant another night would have to be wasted.

Scottsdale was starting to seem very far away.

As he rode Dancer found himself thinking about Daphne Smart. He could not have said why that was so. She was a pretty enough young thing with that mop of red hair and lively green eyes, certainly. She was pleasant to be around. A hard-working spirited girl, but Dancer was not shopping for a companion. He would ride to Scottsdale, conduct his business there and then return home to await whatever was to come next.

Or to his home base — which was what Socorro was. Hardly a home as most men knew one. All the same, he had no room for a woman in his life. And what kind of life was it, anyway? Riding men down, sometimes having to shoot them. Dragging them back to be hanged or jailed or simply scolded by indignant parents. A bunch of mostly petty miscreants on the run from the law or their own shame.

Dancer was again near the small stand of pine trees and he rode into their heavy, dusty shade to cool his horse. He swung down, loosened the twin cinches of his Texas-rigged saddle and squatted down beside his horse with a blade of grass between his front teeth. It was then that he saw them.

Along his backtrail four men rode, and they were not riding at leisure. Frowning, Dancer rose, and squinted into the sunlight, trying to make them out. But he could identify none of them by face or by mount. They could have been anyone, riding anywhere, but

Dancer knew. These were men on a mission, riding their horses harder than was sensible under the high sun.

If they were SS riders they were riding away from where Solon's herd was gathered, but if they were not SS riders, who could they be?

There were a number of men in Dancer's past who would be happy to track him down, but he knew no one in this corner of the territory, in fact had never been in the vicinity before. It had to be someone from the SS. Not Solon, for what reason could he have to ride after Dancer in such haste?

As the four men drew nearer, making their way up the hillslope, Dancer thought he could identify one man. Bulky, huge across his chest, his neck was thick and his arms strained at the fabric of his shirt-sleeves. He had met only one man like that during his brief stay in Matchstick — met him in the Blue Ribbon saloon. It was Bull Brody, he was sure of it. That meant the others were probably his companions on that night. There had been six of them, Dancer recalled, but these four must have been among them. Were they still intent on settling that score?

Dancer tried but failed to identify any of the others as they flagged their horses up the slope below. He tightened the cinches on the bay's saddle while he pondered tactics. He could pick off the lead rider. That would draw the others up; it might also leave Dancer open to a charge of murder placed before a jury which would almost certainly have some SS riders sitting on it.

He could mount the bay and ride like hell toward Matchstick, knowing the men behind him rode tiring horses. But he needed that bay horse for a different reason, and he did not want it to break down, founder. He could fort up where he stood, among the pines and let them try to dig him out, but they might do just that, circling the small stand of trees, firing at intervals until Dancer was dead or driven to surrender.

The last, least promising option was

to try talking to them.

These men would be in no mood for conversation. He had tried that once, in the Blue Ribbon. Dancer saw the lead rider appear over the rim of the slope and he sighed. They were determined to have their fight and he would have to give it to them. He unsheathed one of his Henry rifles, went to a knee and aimed that way. When he triggered off, the rifle bullet flew over the head of the onrushing men as it was intended to, but it was close enough to let them know that it could have lifted their leader out of his saddle.

They immediately reined up and swung their horses away. Dancer could see one of the horses, a gray with its tongue hanging out, balk at the wild halt-and-go spurring of its angry rider. As they disappeared temporarily from Dancer's line of vision, he jacked a fresh cartridge into the receiver of his rifle and muttered to his own horse, 'You're lucky, you know that?' Mistreating a horse that trusted you and which you might need for your very survival was high on Dancer's short list of cardinal sins.

Having started a fight, and with no sensible way to escape, Dancer hunkered down for what might prove to be a prolonged battle, wondering as he did so how a bar fight could have driven his pursuers to this extreme.

It made no difference, he supposed. They were here and looking for blood. Unless they backed off, he could promise them that they would see some blood on this lonely, hot day.

8

'This isn't going to be so easy,' Billy Short said as the four men hunkered down beside their heated horses in an airless arroyo.

'Who ever thought it would be?' Bull Brody grunted. 'The man's a hired gun and he's loaded for bear.'

'Why do we have to take him?' Walt Grange asked. Walt had not been among the SS hands in the Blue Ribbon on that night. He had seldom even talked to Reno Marke or Bull Brody. But from the little that he had been told, he was riding for the brand and this Dancer was some sort of threat to them all. His decision to ride with the gang had been made for that reason and because of the chance to break loose from the tedium of a cowhand's average day. However, this wasn't the kind of excitement he had had in mind.

The man, Dancer, was waiting atop the knoll with a rifle at the ready.

'He's dangerous,' Reno Marke said, looking up from his crouch at Grange. 'He's working for people who mean to take the SS down.'

'Who?' Grange asked, wiping the sweat from his eyes.

'The damned squatters along the Chickasaw and Esperanza del Rio,' Reno Mark fabricated. 'On the one hand they're trying to take all of Mr Solon's land away from him, and if that doesn't work they plan to see that the cattle die of thirst.'

'I didn't know it was that serious,' Grange said. He reached for his canteen, before remembering he hadn't taken the time to bring one along.

'It's that serious,' Reno said. 'Because Dancer is now wearing a badge. How he got it, I don't know.'

'It's a try at forcing the SS out of business,' Bull Brody added, looking up at Grange from under his heavy black eyebrows. 'Besides that, it's personal. I told you about Dancer roughing us up in town.'

'No, but I heard about it,' Grange said.

'That was just the start of it trying to peck around edges, drive off the boys one by one. Any SS man who shows his face in Matchstick from here on is going to get harassed, locked up or killed.'

Grange whistled softly and mopped his sweaty face again.

'Obviously we can't take care of the town marshal in Matchstick; we have to take him now while he's on Solon's land.'

'I can see that,' Grange said, taking both men at their word. 'The question then is: how are we to do it?'

Billy Short, who had remained silent, sweltering in the dry heat of the sage-scented ravine, now spoke up. 'We've got him outgunned,' Short said irritably. 'Why don't we just ride up there and start firing. We're bound to hit him sooner or later, even with all those trees around.'

'Don't get so impatient, Billy,' Reno said. 'Yours is a poor idea. He has position on us, and is more liable to pick us off one by one than we are to hit him.'

Billy Short sulked into silence. He was sitting on the ground, arms looped around drawn-up knees. 'I just want to get moving, doing something before he gets away.'

'The only shot he fired missed by a wide margin,' Grange said. 'Maybe this man isn't all his reputation supposes.'

'He wasn't trying to hit us,' Bull Brody said. 'Dancer's the law now. He felt obligated to fire a warning shot, as the law does.' He rose and stretched his back. 'And that notion is going to get him killed. Because when I shoot I don't play games.'

'Then let's get to it,' Reno Marke said, taking the bridle of his trembling sorrel horse to steady it. 'Which way, Bull?'

'We circle him. Let Dancer sit on that

hill as long as he wants. One thing I'll promise you,' he said, swinging heavily into the saddle. 'He'll never reach Matchstick.'

★ ★ ★

Dancer continued to study the arroyo where his pursuers had taken refuge. They would not remain there long; they could not afford to. Even if he had a good shot at them as they emerged from the gorge, Dancer decided not to take it. For one thing, to kill SS men right now would no doubt infuriate Solon and snuff the barely ignited thought in his mind that he could, should, deal with the Chickasaw settlers rather than start a range war. Also, if Dancer were to kill a few men out here, there would be repercussions for Royce Peebles. How could he have brought in a known killer to do his job?

The shadows were growing longer, though the day gave no indication of fading to coolness yet. Dancer saw the

162

men — four of them — riding up the far side of the arroyo to begin a struggling climb up the rocky slope to the east. Dancer's mouth tightened. He now saw their plan clearly. They meant to circle and block off the road to Matchstick. They would clamber among the rocks and take up their positions for an ambush. At least, that was what Dancer would have planned if he were among them. What could he do, then?

Certainly not turn back, riding farther into SS land. He decided suddenly, thrust his rifle back into its scabbard and mounted the bay again. He was going to ride due west toward the Chickasaw, and from there attempt to make his way back to town by riding the river trail as he had before. While he was there he would have a good opportunity to rest and water his horse and tell Tom Lang and the other men about his meeting with Solon.

The sun was in Dancer's eyes as he left the broken hills and emerged on to the cultivated land adjoining the Chickasaw. He recognized the area and estimated that Tom Lang's parcel was no more than a mile to the north.

An hour later he had crossed Esteban Cruz's sliver of land and was on the Lang ranch.

As he approached the house, he suddenly drew up his horse and his eyes narrowed. There was a strange mount tied up in front of the house. Dancer loosened his holstered guns and rode forward at a walk. He could make out the brand on the flank of the piebald horse now; SS. Frowning, Dancer approached the house, his right-hand pistol clenched in his grip. He didn't like the feel of this.

But as he came nearer Tom Lang stepped out on to the porch, apparently untroubled. With him was a tall, dusky man wearing a holstered Colt low on his hip. Both men studied Dancer's approach. When he was near enough, Dancer called out:

'Howdy, Tom! Everything all right?'

'Well, didn't expect to see you back so soon,' Tom said with seeming cordiality. 'Swing down and meet Smoky Faver — unless you've already met.'

'No, we haven't,' Dancer said, holstering his gun. He stepped out of his saddle and went to the porch.

'You're Dancer,' Smoky Faver said, eyeing him speculatively.

'Mr Faver is the SS foreman,' Tom explained. 'We've been having a little chat. Brian Solon sent him over to ask for a get-together to discuss matters further.'

Dancer was still squinting into the sun. He said, 'That didn't take long. I was just at his house.'

'Mr Solon don't take long to make his decisions,' Smoky Faver said evenly.

'I guess not.'

'So,' Tom said almost joyously, 'I'm going to get the homesteaders together and negotiate with Solon about watering rights.'

'That's fine, Tom,' Dancer said, meaning it. 'I'd like to be there to see it, but right now it's best for you if I pull out of here and try to make my way back to Matchstick.' Dancer was frowning again. 'I've got some men on my back trail,' he said, adding for Smoky Faver's benefit, 'Four SS riders.'

'Why . . . ' Faver scowled darkly. 'What are you thinking, Marshal? That Mr Solon might have sent some men after you?'

'I don't know whether they were sent or not. Bull Brody is one of them. I could make a fairly good guess who the others are.'

'Brody, Reno, Billy Smart,' Faver said, counting on his fingers. 'That would be the ones you gave hell to in town the other night.'

'I didn't give them hell, I just let them look at the gate,' Dancer answered.

'This is their grudge, Dancer,' Faver said. 'I assure you that Mr Solon has not instructed any of his hands to go after you. He would have told me. He is serious about trying to work out a solution to our problems, and not interested in stirring up trouble with the law. Anyone tracking you is doing it on his own — and probably won't have a job on the SS after I report back to Mr Solon.'

Dancer believed the man. He spoke with intensity. Of course the foreman was loyal to Solon, to his men, but there was disapproval in his eyes. If Solon was really ready to try for a peaceful solution to matters, he would hardly send men out to gun down the marshal. That settled matters in Dancer's mind, but did nothing to ensure his safety on his ride back to Matchstick.

'Tell Solon that I don't want to kill any of them — I could have today — but if they keep coming I will show them the back door to hell.'

For a moment Faver stood studying the man in front of him, the cold glow of those gray eyes; then he nodded. 'I'd better be getting back to the home range,' he said. He nodded to Tom and stepped off the porch to swing aboard his piebald horse.

'This may work out well after all, Dancer,' Tom Lang said as they watched Faver ride away into the glare of the low sun. 'Thanks to you. But this other trouble . . . '

'I'm taking it with me, Tom, off your land.'

'All right,' Tom Lang said with a flash of relief. 'We don't need any more trouble, you understand.'

'I do understand,' Dancer said. He returned to his bay horse and mounted up, turning its head toward the river as the sun began to color and sink slowly in the west.

Guiding his horse down the sandy bank he turned the bay's head south toward Matchstick. It was cool along the river, with the sun hidden from view, the flowing water meandering through its course. After an hour the few stray clouds began to capture stolen color from the dying sun and cast pink and violet pennants across the sky. All was peace and coolness along the Chickasaw, but Dancer rode with wariness along the shore.

He was thinking now that his pursuers might have figured what route he was taking, doubled back; that any second the stillness of the dusk could be broken by the racketing shot of a Winchester. And if they were positioned on the banks above him, he would have no chance in a gunfight.

A group of four or five coots took to rapid wing from the water's surface, their black forms flitting across the sky like darting shadows. Passing a twisted sycamore he startled two cottontail rabbits who bounded away from his horse's hoofs. Moments later a sulky-looking coyote slunk past. It must have been stalking the rabbits. It gave Dancer a scathing look as it disappeared into the sumac brush and resumed its hunting.

Purple dusk had settled before Dancer came in sight of Matchstick. He had seen no one; no one seemed to have followed him, but there was still a cautiousness about him as he rode toward the Come Along Stable. The men stalking him were not the sort to give up and go away. They proved that by the length of time they had held their grudge over the night in the Blue Ribbon saloon.

Reaching the stable he rode in, ducking his head to clear the lintel, rather than dismounting outside. A man he did not recognize came forward to meet him.

'Where's Porky?' Dancer asked more sharply than he had intended.

'Over at Sadie's, having some supper. You can trust me with your horse, Marshal.'

'Sure. I'm sorry. I've ridden a long way and I'm kind of tired.'

After removing his rifles from their scabbards he stumped along the dusty street toward the Silver Palace hotel. There were few people on the streets, though the saloons seemed to be doing a rousing business. Dancer kept his eyes moving, surveying the alleyways, the shadows beneath the awnings.

From out of the gloom of dusk a figure rushed toward him. A woman. It was Esperanza del Rio, holding her striped skirt high as she rushed along the street. He stood watching her approach. Panting, she halted before him, touching her fingers to her breast. She was smiling broadly.

'What's the matter? Are you late for work?' Dancer asked.

'Oh,' she said negligently, flipping a hand in the air. 'I don't work at the Blue Ribbon any longer now. I'm just hurrying home.'

'Did those men scare you off the other night?' he asked.

'Drunk men? I see plenty of them. They don't scare me, just make me mad. No, it's not like that it's just that Royce don't want me to work there no more. Besides, I have a big job taking care of him.'

'Royce Peebles is staying with you?'

'Sure! Don't you remember I told you he was going to?'

Dancer had a vague recollection of

that statement. He was curious enough to ask, 'Do you think he'll be coming back to work soon?'

'Not so soon,' Esperanza said, wagging her head though her bright smile remained fixed. 'First he is taking me to Phoenix.'

'To Phoenix?' Dancer asked in puzzlement.

'Yes, to take my claim before the judge there — so that I can recover my land from Solon.'

'Peebles is going along with the idea?'

'But of course! It is what you told me to do, Dancer. Take my land grant to the courts.'

'I also should have made it clear that it might not work.'

'I am right!' she insisted.

'Yes, I know that you are — to your way of thinking, but the judge will have to follow the law of this country, and I don't know how that reads. It might take you a very long time, Esperanza.'

'If so, it does not matter.' She shrugged. 'Royce and I are determined to see it through.'

With that she started on her way at a brisk walk. Dancer watched her go, the hip-swaying motion of her body, her flowing black hair. No wonder she had been able to talk Peebles into seeing it through with her. Yet, Dancer was thinking as he trudged on toward the hotel, if Peebles was going to Phoenix with Esperanza, where did that leave him? Oh, the town would find a new marshal, eventually, but Dancer had no time to waste staying around Matchstick, waiting. He would have to talk to Royce Peebles in the morning, maybe he had already thought this through and had a man in mind to replace him.

Now as he approached the Silver Palace Dancer glanced up toward his room. He could swear that there was a lit lamp there, burning very low. He scowled, remembering Reno Marke and Bull Brody. He doubted that they had simply given up on their search. He supposed they could have found his room easily enough. Dancer slowed his pace still more as he made his approach to the hotel.

He entered the alley to his left and stood peering up at his window. Now he could make out a familiar silhouette in his window. Daphne Smart was peering out into the dark alley. Why? Dancer wondered if she had seen something there, heard a sound. It seemed the only explanation.

Silently he stepped around to the front of the hotel and leaned his Henry rifles against the wall. If there was trouble waiting in the alley it was too dark, and the work would be close for a rifle. Loosening his two revolvers in their holsters, he again stepped to the head of the alley. He saw nothing, but he heard gravel crunching under a boot as someone took a step toward him.

'If you don't want trouble, get out of here,' he called to the darkness. 'This is Marshal Dancer talking.'

'That's all we wanted to know,' a voice answered and they stepped into the band of faint light cast through the window by the lantern in Dancer's upstairs room.

There were two of them. By the vague light, Dancer recognized one of them as the man called Billy. The other he had not seen before. He was young and narrowly built.

'We've been waiting for you, Dancer,' Billy Short said confidently.

'Have you? Men don't usually make that kind of mistake with me,' Dancer answered.

Short chuckled. 'What are you going to do? There's two of us.'

'I can count,' Dancer said in a cold voice.

'Count these then,' Billy Short said as he pawed at his holstered Colt. But Dancer was far too quick for him. He fired twice before Short's gun was even out of the holster, once with each of his guns. Short looked at his chest where the two holes had begun to bleed profusely. Then he dropped his pistol and looked skyward. He might have glimpsed the stars spread across the night sky before he dropped to his face.

The other man, young Walt Grange, stood gawking at Dancer.

'Go ahead,' Dancer told him, reholstering his guns. 'I'll give you a chance. If you don't have the heart for it, I'd ride back to the SS and hope that Brian Solon will give you your job back.'

The youngster hesitated and Dancer bellowed at him. 'I'm not giving you all night to make up your mind!' And Walt Grange, knowing that he was not man enough to stand up against those twin Colts of Dancer, spun on his heel and ran away into the darkness of the alley. After a minute, Dancer heard a horse being ridden away hard, its hoofs thudding against the packed earth.

Dancer returned to the head of the alley where a small group of townspeople, drawn by the commotion, were gathering. Dancer gathered his two rifles and spoke to the gathered citizens.

'What's the marshal generally do with dead men?'

'Hutchins is the undertaker here. He

usually picks up any dead and bills the town later.'

'All right,' Dancer said, 'tell him there's one in the alley he can have.'

A few of the gathered men started to ask questions, but Dancer felt no obligation to contribute to the gossip mill. He stalked to the front door of the hotel, brushed past another small group of onlookers standing there, crossed the lobby and went up the stairs toward his room. Daphne Smart stood in the doorway, looking out at him.

'I heard the shots,' she said, her face so pale her lips were nearly white.

'Yes,' Dancer said, placing his rifles against the wall in the corner again.

'Are you hurt, John? Who was it you shot?'

'I don't think you'd know him,' Dancer said, sitting on the bed. 'And it probably doesn't matter much. One thing I've been thinking, though, Daphne . . . '

'Yes?'

'I don't think you ought to be

hanging around me.'

Daphne stood in stunned silence. She wore a dark blue dress with ruffles on the bottom and at the wrists. She seemed to stagger a little as she backed against the wall to lean against it. Eventually she managed to answer.

'But, John, I want to. I want to be around you very much.'

'You know I'll be leaving soon,' he said as he unbuckled his gunbelt, placed it on the table and thrust his third pistol under the pillow.

'You'd leave . . . the town, just like that?'

'These people aren't helpless,' Dancer said. 'Besides, Royce Peebles will be on his feet soon.'

'He's going to Phoenix.'

Dancer frowned, 'Where'd you hear that?'

'I went by Esperanza's house this afternoon to see how he was doing. She told me. It has something to do with her land grant.'

'Well, Matchstick will just have to

find a new marshal,' Dancer said as he removed the badge from his trail-dirty yellow shirt.

'You're determined to go?'

'Of course. I gave my word.'

'I see. That's important to a man, I know.'

'Especially to one in my business,' Dancer said. 'If I don't keep my word, I'll soon be out of work.'

She moved nearer to him and stood bare inches away, her green eyes studying his face. 'Will you give me your word, John?'

'About what?' he asked, his eyes narrowing.

'That you'll come back and see me after you're finished with your work in Scottsdale?'

'I can't do that, Daphne,' he said gently. 'That job is shaping up to be a difficult one. I don't know if I'll be coming back at all.'

9

Dancer was still thinking about the hurt and anger in Daphne's eyes when she'd left his room the evening before, as he left the hotel and started down the street toward the Come Along Stable. He should have promised the woman something, but how could he? He had told her the truth — there was going to be big trouble in Scottsdale. There was a rough bunch of men waiting for him, and Dancer had no assurance that he would ever be able to visit anyone again — it wouldn't have been a promise he was making her, but only a vague hope.

It seemed slightly cooler on this day. There were thin strands of sheer cloud on the northern horizon, near-formless, substanceless things. A pair of townspeople passed him and raised their hands in greeting. He wondered how they could know him, but then his presence hadn't exactly gone unnoticed in Matchstick.

Dancer sauntered across the street at an angle, heading toward the stable. Inside, the dark building was almost cool. He paused for a moment, letting his eyes adjust, then he made his way to the third stall where his bay horse stood watching him expectantly, its eyes bright in the shadows.

'Porky!' Dancer called out.

'Be right out,' Porky Bing called from somewhere not far away and in a minute the little man came toward Dancer, a small sheaf of papers in his hand. 'Oh, it's you, Marshal. Come to settle up, have you?'

'That's right. If you would ready my horse and take him over to the Silver Palace, I'd appreciate it.'

'Sure thing.' Porky removed his tattered straw hat and scratched at his head. 'A lot of people been looking for you this morning, Marshal.'

'For me?'

'Yes. The mayor, Lew Sheridan, was

here just a little while ago.'

'I don't know him,' Dancer said. 'I've never met the man.'

'Well, he was interested in talking to you about a few things, he said. He told me that he would go over to the marshal's office and wait around for you.'

'You said there were others. Who else wanted to see me?'

'Well, not long after Mayor Sheridan left, Tom Lang came by in his buckboard. I guess he'd taken Dottie over to Nichols' store. She wants to try to work at least a few more weeks. Tom was about as happy as I've ever seen him. He said if I saw you I was to tell you that the small ranchers had a meeting with Brian Solon and it had worked out to everyone's satisfaction — I guess you know what that means.'

'Yes, I do. Thank you.'

'The other man who wanted to see you is probably still hanging around somewhere. I think he went out back to look over my rolling stock.'

Dancer felt a small current of warning run up his spine. Glancing toward the back yard of the stable, visible through a small open door, Dancer asked Porky Bing, 'What's the man's name?'

'I couldn't tell you that, Marshal.' Porky said wagging his head. 'He didn't introduce himself, and I don't know him, but I've seen him around town now and then.'

'How did he look?' Dancer asked.

'Look? Well, thinking it over he looked kind of jittery, nervous maybe. I guess I shouldn't have let him wait around.'

'That's all right. I'll go see what he wants.'

As Porky took Dancer's saddle blanket and carefully smoothed it on the bay's back, preparatory to saddling, Dancer went out the small back door of the stable into the brilliant sunlight, squinting across the yard where buckboards, carriages and freight wagons to be hired stood in an uneven rank. He glanced to his left and then to his right, but still he did not see a thing until the man, appearing as a shadow before the sun-glare opened up with his revolver. The first bullet whipped past Dancer's head and he dove for the ground, rolling under one of the wagons. A second and third shot followed, grooving the wood of the wagon bed, splintering its side.

'Come out of there, gunman!' a somehow familiar voice called, and Dancer, peering out of his shelter, saw a man approaching. 'Let's see how good you really are, Dancer.'

Dancer had landed hard on his right side when he went to the ground, and that arm felt numbed. He slicked his left-hand gun from its holster and waited for the approaching man. He seemed to be reloading his pistol — that was only a guess, since Dancer could see only his adversary's legs. He was in an uncomfortable position, and slithering out to try to rise to his feet would leave him in a vulnerable stance for a few seconds.

'Come out of there, Dancer! Let's do this man to man.' The shooter added a few taunting curses.

Dancer did not respond. He decided to end it now, in his own way. There was no sense letting the enemy set the rules of the game. Lying on his right side, pistol in his left hand, Dancer squinted along the barrel of his gun. His only target was the man's legs, and so he took what was available.

Twice Dancer fired, the black smoke burning his eyes, acrid in his nostrils. Twice he fired, once at each leg of the approaching assassin. The man screamed horribly and Dancer saw both of his shins seem to come apart. He fell like an unstrung marionette; another scream, followed by deep, curse-filled moans, sounded in the yard.

Cautiously, Dancer rolled to the far side of the wagon and got to his feet. He saw Porky peering fearfully out of the stable door, and he gestured the man back. His enemy was down, but might still have teeth. Dancer eased his way around the wagon, the cursing sobs still loud in the empty yard.

The gunman lay clutching uselessly at his legs with both hands. His pistol lay near by in the dust. Dancer walked toward him and booted the pistol away. Then he stood looking down at the badly injured Reno Marke. His legs were positioned unnaturally, splayed out inside his blood-soaked trousers. Dancer's bullets had caught Marke in each shinbone, destroying both of them.

'You just couldn't leave it alone, could you?' Dancer said, and the blond SS rider looked up to spew forth more violent curses, none of which had the power to hurt Dancer. Porky had re-emerged from the stable to peer fearfully in their direction.

'Better call the doctor,' Dancer told him. 'It looks like he's got a double amputation to take care of here.'

Dancer sat on the tailgate of a wagon under the hot sun and waited there until Porky returned with the doctor and a couple of other men, who might have been there to help the doctor carry Reno Marke to his surgery or were simply excited onlookers. Dancer could not decide which, and he really didn't care. He rose and walked to the shocked-looking Porky.

'I'm going to talk to the mayor if he's still at the marshal's office. Will you have someone walk my horse over to the Silver Palace?'

'Sure thing, Marshal,' Porky said. He was hatless; sweat trickled down his brow. 'Man, you sure know how to clean up a town.' He started in to tell all he knew about the trouble Reno Marke had caused in Matchstick, hurrying on stubby legs beside Dancer as he left the stable. Dancer heard only a word here and there. None of what Porky had to say seemed important now.

Reno wouldn't be a lot of trouble from now on. He'd be lucky if he survived to live out his life in an invalid's wheelchair.

* * *

Dancer trudged down the street, rubbing his sore right shoulder. The sun was riding higher and sweat trickled down his neck. He thought the marshal's office would be easy to find, but as time went by he decided he would have to ask someone where it was. He found an old man sitting in a rocking-chair in front of a harness shop, and he stepped up, tilting his hat back.

'Can you tell me where the marshal's office is?'

'You don't know?' the old-timer asked, staring at the badge pinned to Dancer's shirtfront, a smile on his creased face.

'First day on the job,' Dancer said, returning the man's smile.

After receiving simple instructions, Dancer started back uptown. The marshal's office was on a side street, only one block off the main thoroughfare. A cluster of mature cottonwood trees shaded the low adobe building

188

with bars on its windows. Dancer saw no horses in front of the building, but the door stood open. Dancer prepared to pay his first and last visit to the Matchstick marshal's office.

He knocked on the doorframe as he entered. There was a man in a blue town suit sitting behind the desk, in the marshal's chair. His brown hair was thinning, neatly combed. He had large ears and small, sharp eyes.

'You must be Mayor Lew Sheridan,' Dancer said, removing his hat.

'That's right,' the man said rising. He was angular but not thin. He put out his hand. 'Marshal Dancer — it's about time we met.'

'Past time,' Dancer said. 'I'm leaving town, you see.'

'Kind of leaving us in the lurch, aren't you?' Sheridan said, sitting on the corner of the desk.

'I'm sure there are plenty of men who would take the job,' Dancer replied evenly.

'I'm sure there are,' Sheridan said,

one hand folding into a fist with which he banged the desktop. 'Drifting cowboys, young bored men looking for a little excitement, retired men who got tired of sitting around the house . . . none with any experience or the necessary skills for the job.'

'Peebles will be back in no time.'

'Will he? The doctor is not so sure, and anyway, Royce sent me a letter requesting leave to go down to Phoenix. You, however . . . '

'I am on my way to Scottsdale,' Dancer replied thinly. 'I have business there.'

'I understand,' Sheridan said, tugging at an earlobe. 'But all of my thinking is directed toward the town's well-being. We want Matchstick to be a safe, well-regulated town that attracts new citizens. Listen to me, Dancer. I know what you've done for us in only a few days.

'You tracked down the bank robbers, got that scum, Mad Jack Doyle, and returned the stolen money. Many men would have just ridden on with that much cash in hand. On top of that, you settled a long-simmering dispute between the small Chickasaw ranchers and Brian Solon and the SS.'

'The solution was always there,' Dancer pointed out, 'if they had only tried to work it out amicably.'

'But they hadn't, you see. It took your intervention. I understand now that you have also run some of our well-known troublemakers out of town — Billy Short is dead, of course — no loss to this planet, and Walt Grange run off and told not to return.'

Dancer didn't mention Reno Marke. The mayor would find out about the shoot-out at the stable sooner or later. He only wanted to be on his way.

'It wasn't much,' Dancer replied. 'Any decent lawman could have taken care of these matters.'

'I have to disagree,' Sheridan said, rising to face Dancer. 'Royce Peebles has been a good man at this job, but I can't ever imagine him riding to Brian

191

Solon's ranch and somehow persuading him to talk to the Chickasaw settlers. Or taking two armed men in a gunfight. No, Dancer, you are a special man, the kind Matchstick would be proud to have as our marshal. Tell me — how much are you making right now?'

Dancer frowned. He did not like to discuss his business affairs. He shrugged one shoulder and answered, 'I imagine it averages out to around five hundred a month.'

'Five hundred . . . ' the mayor squinted at Dancer, his mouth hung open just a bit.

'On average. I don't work every month, you see. Maybe it's more, maybe less.'

'Well, that stymies Matchstick, I guess. Peebles is making forty-five dollars a month. I was thinking about offering you more. Fifty, perhaps. That must seem downright insulting to you.'

'I don't insult easily. I know you're here for the benefit of your citizens, Mayor, doing the best you can, but . . . ' Dancer started to unpin his badge, but Sheridan stopped him.

'Give yourself a little more time to consider. You can drop off the badge on your way out of town if you decide you have to be going.'

'There's not much more to consider,' Dancer said.

'No, I guess not,' Sheridan answered heavily. 'Can you tell me, Dancer — how long do men in your *profession* last on average? Can they have wives and family? Settle down anywhere?'

'I've got to be going now,' Dancer said without answering the questions that had no answers.

The sun was rising higher, the skies were white without a wisp of cloud as Dancer trudged back toward the Silver Palace. He hated to start a long ride at this time of day. The sun on the desert can wither a man, turn him to leather. It was just as hard on a horse. Nevertheless he had to get to Scottsdale without further delay. He would rinse off a little, gather his few belongings, his rifles and check out of the hotel.

Across the street he saw a familiar figure in a white dress hurrying into the front door of Sadie's restaurant and his heart gave a little twitch. Should he stop in to say goodbye to Daphne Smart, or slip away, saving the unease a meeting would surely cause? Faltering only slightly, he strode on toward the hotel. He hated goodbyes, he had said too many in his life.

He crossed the hotel lobby where only a few people turned to watch him — he had become a familiar sight in his short time in town. The clerk behind the counter lifted a hand and indicated that he wanted to see Dancer, so he started that way, figuring it had to be something about his bill. It wasn't. The smiling clerk handed him a note on which was scrawled:

Dancer, Brian Solon pushed a large herd through to the Chickasaw yesterday, following the corridor we had cleared for him. There was no trouble with anyone on either side. I'd like to thank you somehow. How about coming by for a big barbecue we're planning? We have plenty of beef to eat. Tom Lang.

Dancer smiled and tucked the note away. It was kind of Tom to offer; Dancer was pleased that he wouldn't have to worry about feeding his family from now on, that Solon wouldn't have to use the dangerous Cahuenga trail to get his cattle to water. He wished he did have time to drop by and eat with the Langs and their neighbors, but he needed to be moving on.

Upstairs, he walked to his room, nudged the door open with his toe, found the room empty and unbuckled his gunbelt, tossing it on to the bedside table. The bed had been made; there was fresh water in the pitcher on the dresser. He filled the basin and stripped off his shirt, surprised to find a large purple bruise on his shoulder from throwing himself to the ground to roll under the wagon at the stable. He had had worse — and this could have been a lot worse. It could have been a bullet hole had Reno Marke been a better shot.

He wondered if Marke had survived. He had a notion to visit the doctor's office to find out, but shrugged that off. As he had shrugged off checking to find out how Royce Peebles was coming along. As he had shrugged off Tom Lang's invitation to the barbecue, and seeing Daphne Smart one last time . . .

In an odd way he would miss Matchstick. He had not felt so welcome, so at home, for a long, long time. His lifestyle was hardly conducive to making friends or to long relationships.

Rinsing off, he continued to study his face in the mirror. Then, at one point, he suddenly and unexpectedly found himself unable to hold his own gaze. Muttering a small curse, he wadded up the face cloth and tossed it down. Dancer grabbed his shirt and buttoned it on. Something was wrong . . .

He saw the shadow from the corner of his eye and spun. Bull Brody was there, his massive shoulders and chest filling the doorway. Brody's head hung forward, his jaw loose.

'Hello, Dancer,' the apelike man said. He trudged forward into the room, closing the door behind him. Dancer backed away a step, his eyes flitting toward the bed where his gunbelt rested. Too far away to do him any good. Damnit! He was losing his edge. What was the matter with him?

'No guns?' Brody said. 'Good. I like it better this way.' He unbuckled his own gunbelt. Brody pushed up on his sleeves and formed an expression he must have meant to be a smile. 'I'm going to beat you to death, Dancer.'

The giant SS rider strode forward, the floor creaking under his weight. Dancer put his fists up defensively and waited. There was little else that he could do. Brody was close enough now that Dancer could smell the stink of whiskey on him, and he struck out with his left fist, catching Brody on the throat. The big man didn't even slow down. When he drove his own fist down, Dancer rolled his head aside and took it on the shoulder. It was like being hit with a sledge-hammer.

Dancer had backed up against the wall, but he realized now that he had to move. There was even more power and muscle under Brody's shirt than he had imagined as a second stunning blow drove into Dancer's body, below his last rib. Dancer's liver screamed a complaint.

Dancer ducked, stepped aside and jabbed out at the brutish Bull Brody's face three times. Now the man had blood streaming from his nose, but Brody was implacable. Relentlessly the bigger man stalked Dancer, his arms held low. Only now and then would he trigger off one of his heavy blows, and when he did there was nothing Dancer could do to avoid them. Dancer continued to jab and move, once catching the shelf of Brody's jaw with a right hand shot which would have floored many a man. It did nothing even to slow Brody's assault. Brody grunted with mild surprise, and that was it. It was something like boxing a grizzly bear. Dancer had to rethink his tactics.

Ducking under a windmilled right-hand blow from Brody, Dancer came up on the other side of Bull. There was a brief moment while the big man reset himself when Dancer had an opening, and he fired rights and lefts, up and down Brody's massive body, using all the strength of his shoulders. It did nothing to slow Bull Brody's murderous attack.

Brody now stood in front of the window, the light curtains drifting around him, nudged by the desert wind. Dancer took another solid punch to the head and staggered a little. Then he moved toward the big man, wanting to get inside of the arc of his swing, where he could not muster power.

It did little good. If Brody had less

space, his animal strength was still overpowering as he muttered muffled curses, grunting each time he landed a blow on Dancer's battered body. Dancer glanced once toward his guns, but the bed seemed miles away and he knew that Brody would never let him get that far.

The two men stood toe to toe, Dancer fighting desperately, Bull landing his methodical trip-hammer punches. Dancer took the one opportunity he thought he had. He charged Bull Brody, lowered his shoulder and tipped him over the window sill. Bull's eyes opened wide as the back of his legs struck wood and he felt himself toppling into space. One meaty hand reached out and snatched the front of Dancer's yellow shirt. He held it in his grip as he fell backward, taking Dancer with him on a spiraling drop toward the floor of the alley two stories below.

10

Dancer struggled up out of a tunnel of darkness, clawing his way toward consciousness. When he had managed it, he was sorry he had. The sun was hot and glaring, the alley breathless. His right wrist felt like someone had set it on fire. When he moved it tentatively, he could feel — hear! — bone grating against bone. He had broken it in the fall. His head still swirled, but he needed to sit up. That proved to be more difficult than he'd anticipated. The ground beneath him was uneven, lumpy.

As Dancer's vision cleared and his dazed mind regained focus he realized that he was lying in the dusty alley on top of Bull Brody. Brody was looking directly at him. But his eyes did not blink as the sun shone full on his face, and his neck was twisted at an impossible angle. Dancer forced himself to move, enough to sit up at least.

That was where they found him: sitting on top of Bull Brody's corpse, cradling his broken wrist in his left hand.

Several passers-by, whose names he did not know, helped him to the doctor's office.

'You'll be able to play the violin again — in time,' the doctor said. Then he smiled. 'A little office humor, Marshal; forgive me.' Then the man's smile faded as he examined Dancer's wrist with thumb and fingers. 'How's the pain now?'

'Not so bad,' Dancer said. The doctor had given him three white pills which Dancer suspected were either morphine or opium, and the pain had abated to a dull hurt, no worse than a bruise.

'I'm going to have to rearrange a few bones, Marshal. You've got a couple in the wrong place and a couple shattered. What were you doing, diving out of a hotel window?'

'Trying to stay alive,' Dancer said with a yawn. The pills, whatever they were, were doing their job. He was given a small windowless room in the rear of the doctor's office and fell on the narrow bed there. He was not hurt that badly now, he thought, closing his eyes. His hand had quit throbbing and he barely felt the ache in his ribs. He had caught a glimpse of his face in the mirror on the wall. A few bruises, one strip of sticking plaster across his jaw. He was a lucky man, he considered. Taken all in all, John Dancer thought himself a very lucky man.

He slept until returning pain nudged him awake. Without a window he could not gauge the time, but he could hear people up and about in the doctor's office. As he swung his feet to the floor, the doctor himself arrived, holding a glass of water in one hand and three white pills in the other.

'I thought you'd be waking up soon. How is the pain?'

'It's bearable,' Dancer said with a

smile, 'but I'd rather not bear it.'

He took the pills the doctor offered him and swallowed them, nodding his thanks.

'You've had visitors this morning,' the doctor told him.

Dancer's first thought was of Daphne, but the doctor told him: 'Mayor Sheridan came by to see how you were doing. After him Tom and Dottie Lang were here to ask about you, along with Esteban Cruz. Royce Peebles looked in. He and Esperanza are on their way to Phoenix. They had just come from the church — they're married.'

'I've had bigger surprises,' Dancer told the doctor, who smiled.

'Oh, and Brian Solon came here to see you.'

'Solon? I wonder what he wanted. Did he seem angry?'

'No,' the doctor said, 'he asked me to thank you for culling his herd. Said you saved him a lot of trouble. Do you know what he meant?'

'I think so,' Dancer said. Apparently

the SS owner hadn't been too fond of Bull Brody, Reno Marke and their friends.

'He also said to tell you that for the first time in years he hadn't lost a single head of beef on his drive to the Chickasaw.'

'Fine,' Dancer said, yawning as the pain pills began to work. 'Do you think I'm in shape to go out to eat breakfast at Sadie's?'

'No. Do you?' the doctor replied.

'I guess not,' Dancer answered. His legs felt very heavy. His head seemed to want to tilt to one side on its own. He lay back on the bed.

'Tomorrow I can let you go home,' the doctor said. 'Today I think you just ought to get some more rest. If you're hungry I can have a tray sent over from Sadie's.'

'I'm not . . . ' Dancer started to say, for his appetite had vanished, but he changed his mind.

'That sounds good. Have someone from there come over with breakfast.'

The doctor nodded as if he had no idea what Dancer was trying to accomplish. 'I'll see to it,' he promised. Then he left the room. Out front a child was crying, a mother trying to comfort it.

Days, seconds, hours passed; in Dancer's tranquilized state he had no idea how long he had been asleep, when the door opened and the small redheaded woman stood beside the bed holding a tray with a red-checked napkin spread over it. She set it down on a bedside table.

'Daphne,' Dancer smiled and tried to stand up.

'Let your head clear before you try that,' Daphne Smart said in a stiff voice. Was she angry with him? 'Would you like some coffee?'

Without waiting for an answer she poured a cup of steaming coffee from a pint-sized pot, handed it to Dancer and seated herself in a wooden chair beside the bed. She folded her hands demurely on her aproned lap. Dancer was unable to read her eyes.

'Thanks for bringing this,' Dancer said.

'Any excuse to get out of the restaurant for a few minutes,' she said. Was that what they had come to? And whose fault was it? 'I could have brought you a breakfast, but the sun's nearly down and the cooks were busy with the supper crowd — I brought a steak and some boiled potatoes.'

'That'll be fine,' Dancer muttered. There were things to say, but he could not think of what they were at this moment, when his mind was still foggy. Sitting on the edge of the bed he sipped the coffee and studied Daphne, who seemed not to have even moved.

'Has anyone come to see you?' she asked.

'A lot of folks. I was asleep when they came, but Doc told me — Mayor Sheridan, Royce Peebles and Esperanza, the Langs and Esteban Cruz. Even Brian Solon, believe it or not.'

'You made a lot of friends in

Matchstick very quickly.' She still did not meet his gaze.

'What's the matter, Daphne?'

'The matter?' Now she did look at him, but those green eyes kept their secrets. 'Why should anything that happens in Matchstick matter to you, John? You're still determined to go on to Scottsdale.'

'Not with a broken wrist,' he said.

'Well, soon then.'

'I don't know. I just might have to forget that job and return the money I was paid.'

'You told me you never returned the fee, succeed or fail.'

'Yes, well, this one is kind of different. I never even made an honest effort to earn my fee. I don't work that way. I've always done my best.'

'So you don't intend to go to Scottsdale?' she asked hesitantly, trembling as she waited for his response.

'No. I guess I don't. I have some money tucked away in Socorro — I can live on that for quite a while. I could have it sent over here.'

'Oh, is that your idea now? To stay in Matchstick for a while?'

'For a little while, at least. Maybe until Peebles gets back from Phoenix.'

'I don't think Royce Peebles is coming back — at least not in the way you mean.' To Dancer's frown, she added. 'He's not in real good shape, you know. I heard that Sanford Wilkes has offered to teach him the banking business. He said he wants to make sure he's never held up again, and he figures with Royce, a former marshal, as a teller, his chances will be much improved.'

'That's a little surprising,' Dancer said.

'I think Esperanza was behind it. She doesn't want her new husband to be a town marshal any more. Not after what happened.'

'No, I can understand that,' Dancer said, standing as Daphne also rose to her feet. 'What about you? What would you think in that situation, Daphne?'

'I think I would be about the happiest woman in the world if my man were the marshal in Matchstick,' she said shakily. There was a moistness in her eyes as she lifted her sleeve and polished Dancer's badge with it, then folded up in his arms.

Dancer whispered to her, 'Anything to keep a lady happy,' and he kissed her. Never had making a bad decision felt so good.

THE END